THE KING BEHIND THE PICTURE

The King Behind the Picture

The story of a boy during the German occupation of Jersey

ELSP

Published in 2013 and reprinted in 2014
by ELSP
11 Regents Place
Bradford on Avon
Wiltshire   BA15 1ED

Origination by Seaflower Books
www.ex-librisbooks.co.uk

Cover design by Brian Cross   iD Design   01534 618698

Printed by CPI Group (UK) Ltd
Croydon, CR0 4YY

2013 © Marianne Le Boutillier (text)
2013 © Pam Du Val (Illustrations)

ISBN 978-1-906641-62-7

All enquiries and correspondence regarding
this book should be directed to
mruthleb@gmail.com

For Frankie-Rose and Stanley

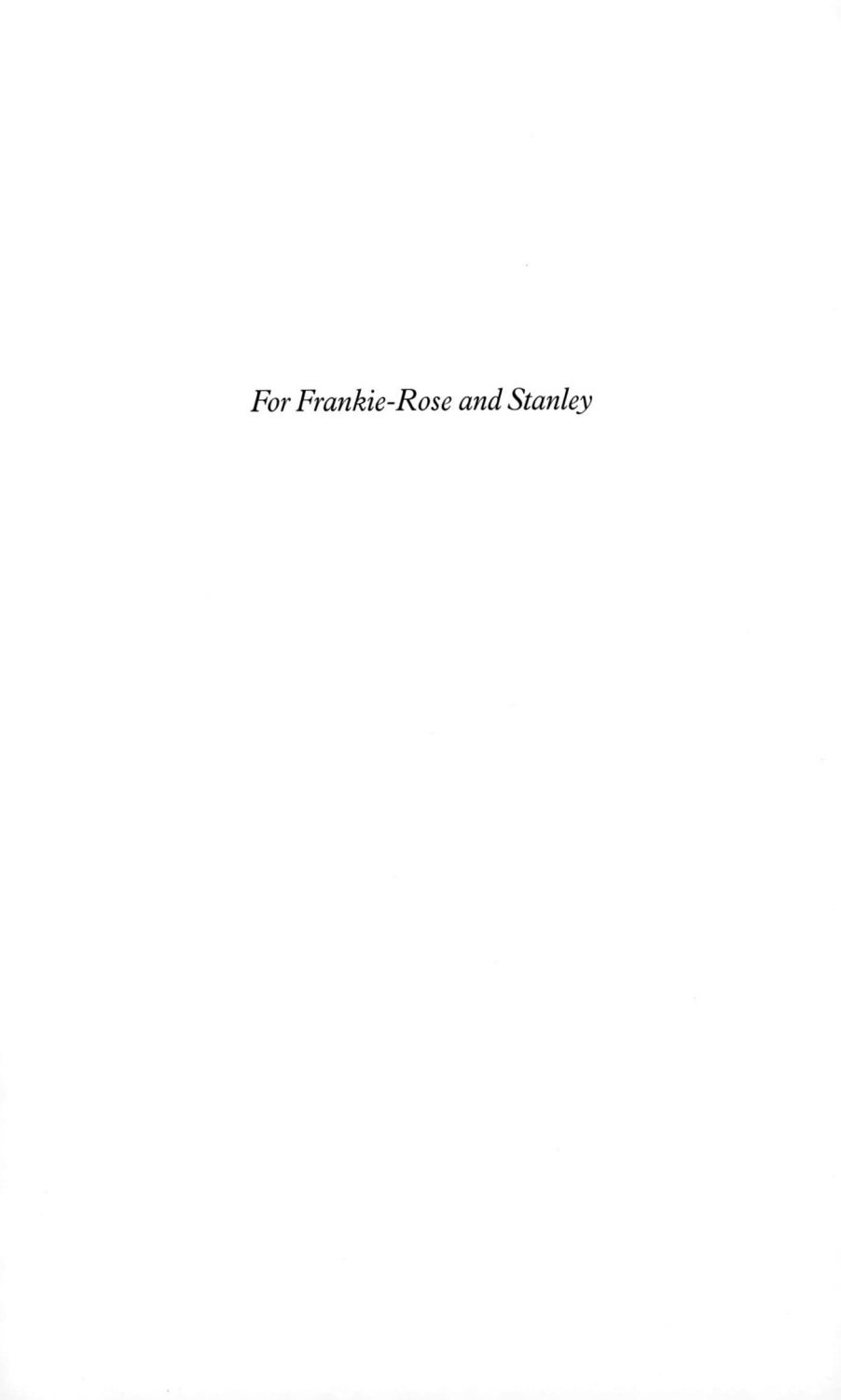

Contents

Chapter 1	What's happening?	11
Chapter 2	Goodbyes	21
Chapter 3	More People Leave	29
Chapter 4	Occupation	38
Chapter 5	Rules! Rules! Rules!	49
Chapter 6	A Trip to Town	59
Chapter 7	Hide That Pig!	73
Chapter 8	Life at School	83
Chapter 9	Gone Fishing	99
Chapter 10	Jack is Sick	108
Chapter 11	Scratch Goes Missing!	120
Chapter 12	The Man in the Woods	129
Chapter 13	Happy Christmas Everyone!	145
Chapter 14	We're Free!	158
Author's Note		179

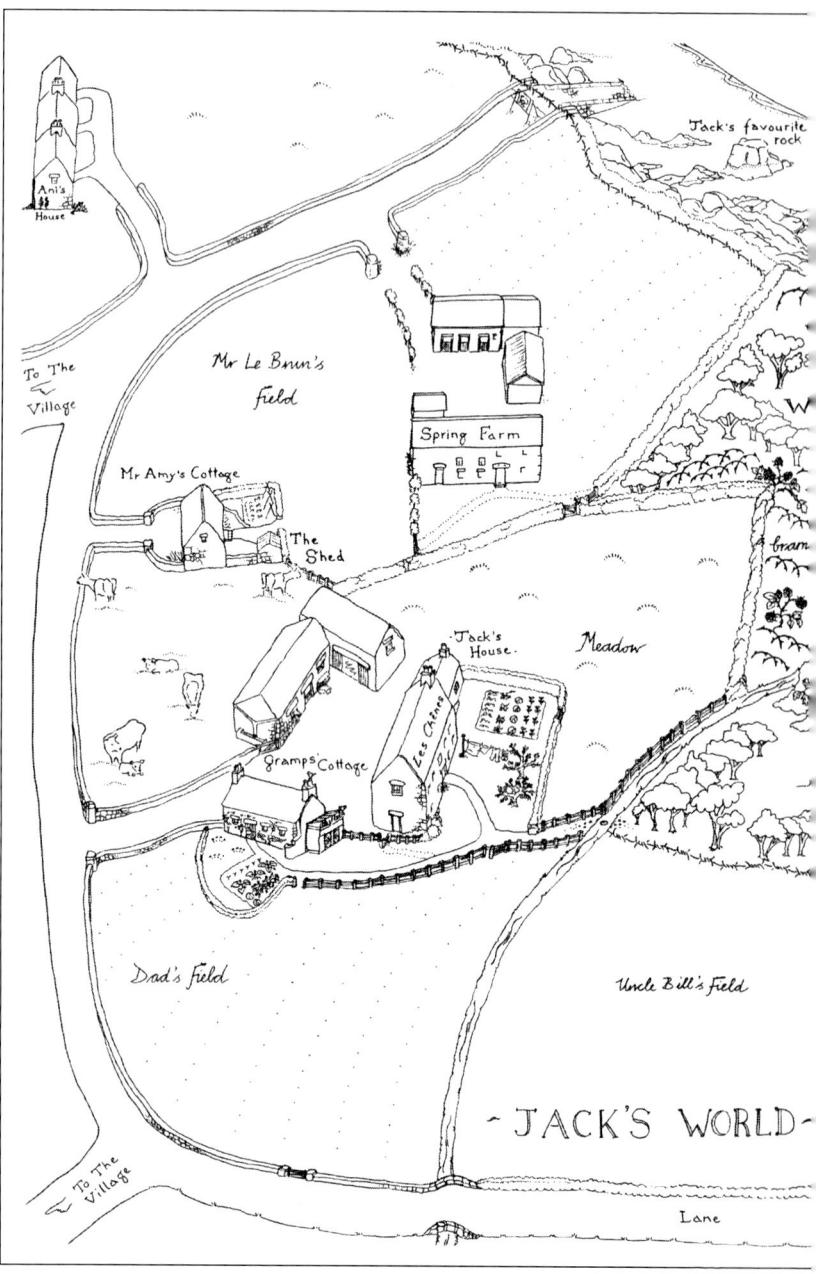

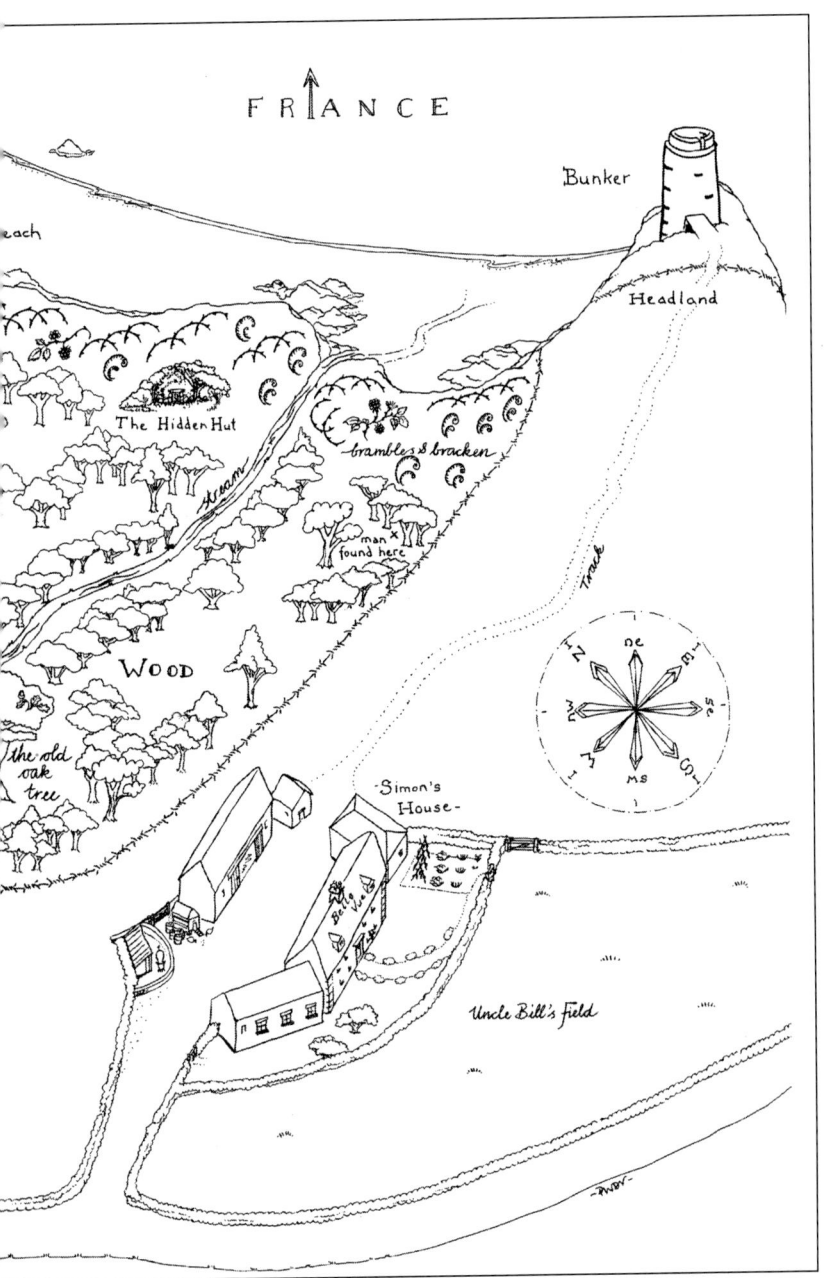

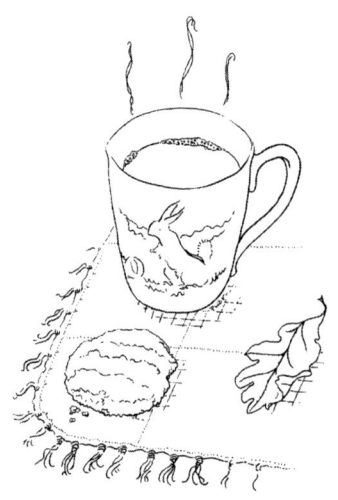

Chapter One

What's happening?

Jack peered into the rock pool searching for little prawns to take home for tea. They were very difficult to see as the bright sunlight shone on the glistening water. He gently poked some slimy seaweed with his fishing net, hoping that the prawns would come out from their hiding place. Then, all of a sudden, he heard someone calling his name. He looked up to see his cousin Simon scrambling over the rocks towards him, with Scratch, his black and white collie dog, following close behind.

'Jack, you've got to look after Scratch – just until we get back,' called Simon, who was out of breath and looked very hot and bothered. 'You will look after him, won't you?'

'Why? What are you talking about, Simon?' Jack asked, putting down his net and stroking Scratch, who jumped up sending water and sand all over him.

'We're leaving Jersey tomorrow; I heard Mum and Dad talking in the stable while I was collecting the eggs.'

'No you're not!' exclaimed Jack.

'Yes we are! We're going to Manchester.'

'Where's Manchester?'

'It's the big city in England where my Auntie Sue lives,' answered Simon. Jack frowned, wondering why Simon would make up such a story.

'I don't believe you!' he said.

'We are! Mum was crying and I looked round the corner and saw her wiping her eyes on her apron. Then Dad touched her face and said that it wouldn't be for long and we could stay with her sister Sue in Manchester.'

'What did she say?' asked Jack.

'She said that it would be very hard for us to leave all our friends behind.'

'You can't go. Who will look after the animals on the farm? You're making it up.'

'I'm not, I'm not!' said Simon, as he began to cry. 'He really did, Jack.' Simon sat down on a rock, sniffed and wiped his eyes, then looked pleadingly at Jack. 'When we go, I want you to look after Scratch. Please!'

Scratch put a paw on his knee and licked his hand and Simon stroked his pet's soft fur. Jack watched. 'It couldn't be true, could it?' he thought. He picked up his net and bucket and marched up the beach towards the lane.

'I still don't believe you, Simon,' he shouted, without looking back.

'Come back!' cried Simon. 'It's true, I promise.'

Jack took no notice and ran up the lane, across the field and squeezed through a hole in the hedge. Then he ran through the trees and bushes in the woods until he reached a big old oak tree. He climbed into its branches and looked back towards the beach. This was his very own thinking place where he came whenever he wanted to be alone. Sometimes he came here when he was happy and just enjoyed looking at the deep blue sea and the coast of France just fifteen miles away. Sometimes, like today, he came when he felt angry and didn't know what to do.

He thought about everything that had happened during the past few weeks. His Mum, Dad and his grandparents, Maman and Poppa, had been very, very serious and wouldn't tell him what was going on. The grownups stopped talking when he came into the room, or whispered so that he couldn't hear and even his big sister Lizzie didn't seem to know what was happening. He felt very confused and rather scared.

Simon wasn't just his cousin, he was his best friend. They were both eight years old and always did things together. Now, he said he was leaving Jersey. Jack wondered whether his family would be leaving the island too. Nothing made any sense at all.

Suddenly he heard a deep booming sound in the distance. It was the third time that morning that he had heard it. It was rather like a thunder clap but longer, like a deep rumbling, grumbling sound. He climbed higher into the tree, peered into the distance and saw huge clouds of dark grey smoke on the horizon somewhere on the coast of France. 'What is it?' he said out loud, staring as the smoke moved higher and higher until it disappeared in the clouds. 'I'm going to ask my Mum what's happening; she's got to tell me.'

He jumped down from the tree and ran through the woods, then splashed across a little stream until

he reached the path leading to Les Chênes, the farm where he lived with Mum, Dad, ten year old Lizzie and baby Thomas. He saw Maman and Poppa, who were chatting outside their little cottage in the yard and waved to Dad as he lifted barrels full of potatoes into the back of the lorry, ready to take to the harbour to be shipped to England. Then he found Mum in the garden taking in the washing and baby Thomas, who was lying on a rug looking up at the sheets as they blew in the breeze.

Jack threw down his net and bucket and ran to Mum, flinging his arms around her waist.

'Hey, Jack, what's all this about? It's not like you to want a hug,' she said, wrapping her arms around her son. But all he could say was, 'what's happening Mum?'

Mum could tell that Jack was very upset, so she asked Lizzie, who was leaning out of her bedroom window watching all that was going on, to come down and take Thomas indoors. Lizzie soon appeared, picked up her brother and took him into the kitchen.

"Come on, my love, tell me what's wrong,' Mum said, in a quiet, gentle voice.

'Simon said that he's going to England,' he whispered, really hoping Mum would say that Simon had made it all up.

'Yes, they leave tomorrow,' she replied, hugging him tight. Jack thought for a moment, and then looked up at his Mum.

'Are we going too?' he asked with a little shaky voice.

'No, your father and I have decided to stay.'

'Why do they have to go then?' he cried.

'Simon's mother is English and it's not safe for her to stay here. They're going to stay with her sister. We'll look after Uncle Bill's cows, pigs and hens until they come back again.'

'I don't understand! Why can't she stay with us?'

'You've heard us talk about the war, Jack. The German army is fighting in France and the English are fighting against them, so it's better that all the English people go back to England now,' Mum answered, hugging him close again.

'Can I look after Scratch?'

'Of course you can,' Mum replied. 'You'll enjoy looking after him, won't you?' Jack nodded. Then he had a terrible thought, pulled away from his mother's arms and looked deep into her eyes.

'Are the German soldiers coming here, Mum?'

Mum looked very serious and said, 'Yes, I think they

are. The German army is not far away from us now. Did you hear the rumbling sound coming from the French coast this morning?'

'Yes, and I saw some smoke too,' replied Jack.

'That terrible sound and the smoke you saw, is from the tank fire and exploding bombs that the Germans are using to fight the French army,' explained Mum.

'I saw planes flying towards France. Are they dropping bombs too?' asked Jack.

'Yes, the British RAF planes are trying to stop the Germans because they don't want them to get as far as England.' She stopped and sighed. 'But I don't think they can stop them coming to Jersey, Jack. I think they could land here very soon.'

'But there are lots of British soldiers here to keep them out,' said Jack, his voice beginning to sound very scared. 'All the grownups and children could fight too. Then they would have to leave us alone.'

'If only it was that easy love,' said Mum. 'The Germans have ships with guns, planes with bombs and thousands of soldiers. I don't think we could win, do you? Anyway the British soldiers are leaving.'

'Why?' Jack exclaimed.

'Winston Churchill, you know, the Prime Minister in London, has decided that it would be safer for us to surrender peacefully,' explained Mum.

Jack didn't even know what surrender meant! All he knew was that he didn't like the sound of this at all.

'What do you mean, surrender?' he asked.

'Well, if the German army is determined to occupy Jersey and the British soldiers try to stop them, the German planes might bomb our homes until we give up and let them in. A lot of people could get killed, Jack, and nobody wants that.' Jack frowned and tried hard to understand.

'So the British soldiers are going back to England, then the Germans can land without fighting, and no one will be killed,' he said.

'That's right. We don't want them here, but it seems that all we can do is surrender,' answered Mum.

That was not what Jack wanted to hear. He wanted his Mum and Dad to say that everything would be alright and the Germans would never land on his island. He wanted to play on the beach and go fishing with Simon. He even decided that he wouldn't mind if Lizzie teased him and Thomas messed up his games. He wanted things to stay just as they were.

'Mum, what will happen to us?' he whispered.

'I don't know, but the war should be over by Christmas, at least that's what we've been told,' Mum answered quietly. She took his face in her soft warm hands and looked into his eyes. 'Most of all, Jack, you must remember that we've got each other. We're a family – you, me, Dad, Lizzie, Thomas, Maman and Poppa. Whatever happens we'll stay together. We'll be just fine, you'll see.'

Mum smiled, ruffled his light brown hair and gave him a big hug, then led him into the kitchen for a cup of hot milk and his favourite ginger biscuit. Jack was frightened, but knew that whatever happened, he would never be alone.

Chapter Two

Goodbye

The next day it was time to say goodbye to Simon and his family. Everyone was very upset. When supper was over and baby Thomas was asleep, Maman and Poppa came to babysit. Maman looked tired and sad. She had always had her sons living nearby, John across the yard with his wife Jane and their children, and Bill with May, Simon and Clare up the hill at their farm called Belle Vue. She couldn't imagine what life would be like when half her family left the island. She took hold of Poppa's hand and squeezed it tight.

'Give everyone a hug and tell them that we'll miss them,' she called as John, Jane Lizzie and Jack walked up the drive towards Bill's farm.

'Tell them we love them and hope they'll be home very soon,' said Poppa.

'We will,' called back Mum with a wave and a smile.

'Come on, old girl,' said Poppa, patting Maman's hand. 'Let's go. We can listen to the news on the wireless. Maybe we can find out a bit more about this dreadful war.'

Jack and Lizzie ran ahead of their parents and soon arrived at Belle Vue. The first thing they saw was Simon closing a cage balanced on a small hand cart. From inside the cage, there were squawking and scratching sounds and very loud quacks, as the three hens, two ducks and Hubert the cockerel protested angrily at being captured in such an undignified manner. Scratch was running backwards and forwards barking and wondering what was going on.

'They're for you to look after,' explained Simon. Then he poked Jack on the arm. 'Do you believe me now?' he asked. Jack nodded.

'Sorry Simon,' he said, feeling a bit ashamed of himself. 'I'll look after Scratch, I promise.'

'You'll take him to the beach won't you, Jack?' asked Simon.

'Of course I will – every single day,' he replied.

Simon sighed. 'I wanted to take him with me, but Dad said that no pets are allowed on the boat. It's not fair.'

Jack didn't know what to say, so he was pleased that just then Uncle Bill came out of the henhouse carrying a cardboard box.

'Hello Jack, look in here,' said Uncle Bill. 'Can you take care of these baby chicks for us?'

'Oh yes, Uncle Bill,' Jack replied, picking up a fluffy yellow chick. It looked so small sitting in the palm of his hand and he stroked it gently. 'Come and see, Lizzie,' he called and she ran over to have a look.

'They're beautiful!' she said as she peered into the box where eight more yellow bundles of fluff scampered about making little chirruping sounds. 'Can I help too?' she asked.

'Of course you can, I'm sure they'll soon settle down in your meadow,' said Uncle Bill as he put the box onto the cart. Lizzie and Jack looked at each other and grinned. This was a job that they would really enjoy!

'There's a lot to do, so why don't you go and help

Aunt May with the packing?' suggested Uncle Bill.

Lizzie and Jack went inside to join Mum, who was already in the kitchen. It was usually such a happy friendly place, with its old black range that made the room warm and cosy in the winter and scorching hot in the summer. But today the fire in the range was out. Even the old kettle, normally whistling, begging someone to make a pot of tea, was quiet.

The table was piled high with boxes of every shape and size, and five year old Clare was watching her mother as she wrapped a china jug in pieces of newspaper and packed them in a box. Aunt May looked up and smiled. 'Hello, have you come to help?' she asked.

'Yes, Aunt May, but why are you packing everything up?' asked Lizzie, 'I thought you were only going for a few weeks.'

'We really don't know how long we'll be gone,' answered Aunt May.

'Mum said that the war should be over by Christmas, then you can come back again,' said Jack.

'Yes, that's what we hope, but actually nobody knows how long it will last.'

Jack glared at his mother. 'You told me it would be over by Christmas, Mum.'

'I know, Jack. I'm sorry. That really is what some

people say, but no one knows for sure,' she answered sadly, putting her hand on his shoulder.

'Why can't you take everything with you, Aunt May?' asked Lizzie.

'We're only allowed to take one suitcase each. There will be lots of people on the boat and not much room for luggage.'

'So what will you do with everything else?'

'Your Mum and Dad will look after a few very precious things, and we will leave most of our furniture here. I hope it will all be safe until we return.' Aunt May sighed. 'Well, let's get on with it. Lizzie, could you help Clare choose three toys to put in her suitcase please?'

Lizzie nodded. 'Come on, Clare,' she said.

'We're going to England on a big boat,' Clare said excitedly as they climbed up the stairs. She was too young to understand that she would have to leave nearly everything behind.

'Jack, can you go into the sitting room and fetch all the family photographs for me please?' asked Aunt May.

Jack went to find them and he looked at the photos on the mantelpiece, the piano and the wall by the window. There were pictures of Aunt May and Uncle Bill's wedding; of Simon and Clare; Maman and Poppa when they were young and lots of very old fashioned people he did not recognise. He took them into the kitchen and wondered which ones Aunt May would choose to take to England. After a few minutes she chose two and put the rest in a box.

'I'll have to keep the pictures up here in my mind,' she said, her eyes filling with tears that trickled down her cheeks.

Jack felt rather embarrassed to see his aunt cry, so he noisily scrunched up some newspaper and gave it to his mum who was packing up a beautiful vase.

'Thank you, son,' she said.

Soon everything was done. Clare had chosen her toys and the suitcases were full and loaded into the car.

'Hurry up! It's time to go,' called Uncle Bill. Everyone put on their coats and took one last look at their home. Aunt May, Mum and Lizzie cried as they hugged each other and said goodbye and Clare clung to her mother looking quite bewildered.

'I'll pray that God will keep you safe until this awful war is over. Make sure that you write to us when you arrive in Manchester,' said Mum.

'We will,' Uncle Bill replied as he locked the front door. 'Chin up, we'll get through this.' Dad took the key and put it into his pocket.

'I'll move the cattle into my fields in the morning. Robin can join Chestnut in the meadow. Don't worry, we'll manage won't we, Jack?' said Dad.

Jack nodded; he would enjoy looking after Robin, the big old farm horse. 'And I'll come to feed the pigs every day,' he said, looking up at his uncle.

'Good lad,' said Uncle Bill. 'Come on, Simon, if we don't hurry up there might not be any room for us on the boat.'

Simon knelt down beside Scratch and flung his arms round the collie dog's neck for the last time. He buried his head in his black and white fur and breathed in the doggie smell, telling his brain to remember it always.

'You be good, Scratch, I'll miss you,' he said as he began to cry.

'Come here, son,' said Uncle Bill gently, pulling him up, taking the lead out of his hand and giving it to Jack. 'You'll see Scratch again soon. Get in the car now, Simon. Come on, let's go.'

'Remember that Scratch loves to be scratched behind his ears,' Simon called between his sobs as he climbed into the little black car.

'I will,' Jack replied.

'I'll leave the car at Frank's shop; you can collect

it from him. Bye everyone!' said Uncle Bill, and with that he honked the horn and drove off up the drive, with Simon and Clare waving furiously through the back window. Scratch whined and tugged on his lead desperate to follow the car.

'You can't go with them, Scratch,' said Jack kneeling down beside the unhappy dog and tying the lead to the cart. 'I'll look after you.'

'It's not fair! I don't want them to go,' cried Lizzie, waving with both hands until the car was out of sight.

'I know, none of us want them to go, Lizzie,' said Mum sadly. 'Come on you two, you bring the cart and we'll see you at home.'

The children watched as Mum and Dad climbed into the lorry loaded with all their aunt and uncle's precious belongings and drove towards Les Chênes. Then they took hold of the cart's long handles and began to pull its noisy cargo of hens, chicks and ducks back to the farm. Scratch whined and pulled on his lead, but the children didn't even notice. They were lost in thought, wondering what would happen to them now.

Chapter Three

More People Leave

The next day everyone seemed very quiet, except Dad, who kept shouting at the children and slamming the doors. This made baby Thomas cry, and even Lizzie and Jack were rather scared as they had never seen their Dad so angry.

'Just keep out of his way,' advised Mum.

Jack frowned. 'But why is he shouting at me when I haven't done anything wrong?'

'Well, he's worried about Uncle Bill and hopes that the family will get to Manchester safely. I'm sure they'll write to us soon to tell us they have arrived. Then he will feel a bit better. He also sometimes wonders whether we should have gone to England too,' answered Mum.

'Why didn't we then?' asked Lizzie, who had come to join them.

'Who would look after Maman and Poppa if we left? We have the cattle and hens to look after and there are Uncle Bill's animals to feed too.' The children agreed, maybe it was right to stay at home.

'Oh, here he comes now,' said Mum. 'Remember what I said; just keep out of his way.' So Lizzie sat on the rug with Thomas tickling him to make him laugh and Jack took Scratch into the sitting room. He watched through a crack in the door as Dad came into the kitchen and took off his Wellington boots, throwing them into a corner. Then he put on his shoes and jacket, took his cap off the peg by the door and went out again without saying a word.

'He's gone, Jack!' called Mum. 'You can come out now!' This made Jack laugh and he went to the window to watch his father as he cycled up the drive.

'Where's he going?' he asked.

'He's going to collect Uncle Bill's car from Uncle Frank's. I hope he'll have a good chat with his big brother and then he might feel a bit better.' answered

Mum.

'A lot better you mean!' said Lizzie.

'Yes, a lot, a lot, a lot!' laughed Jack.

'I agree!' said Mum, smiling at her two children. 'Well, I think you both need something useful to do, so why don't you go and pick some strawberries. If you pick enough, Maman might make some jam.'

The two children thought this was a brilliant plan, they loved Maman's jam! They fetched a big wicker basket to put the strawberries in and ran outside, where they saw Scratch asleep in the sunshine.

'Scratch, come and play' called Jack. But Scratch looked at him with his big sad eyes and didn't move. Jack stroked the collie dog and scratched him behind his ears. 'Poor Scratch, I miss Simon too you know. I hope you'll cheer up soon.' He threw a stick across the yard. 'Fetch Scratch, fetch!' But the unhappy dog just lifted up his head, then put it on his paws again. Lizzie picked up the stick and waved it high above her head.

'Come and get it,' she called encouragingly. Scratch sat up, he really did want that stick!

'Go on,' said Jack, giving him a push. Suddenly, Scratch wagged his tail, barked and bounded towards Lizzie jumping up to get the stick.

'Clever boy, that's better,' she said, throwing it into

the field. As Scratch raced after his new toy, the two children laughed – Scratch would be just fine! Scratch thought so too. Maybe life at Les Chênes wouldn't be so bad after all!

Lizzie and Jack went to pick the lovely ripe strawberries that grew by a red brick wall in the garden. They ate the juiciest ones, and put the rest in their basket. When it was full, they took it back to their warm cosy kitchen where Mum was busy washing the dishes and Maman was sitting by the stove, knitting a long blue and white scarf.

Mum turned as they came in through the door. 'Let's see how many you've picked,' she said as Lizzie held up the basket. 'That's good. What do you think, Maman? Are there enough to make some jam?' she asked.

Maman put down her knitting as they took the basket to her. 'Well done! That's plenty. I'll make some tomorrow and you can help me if you like.'

Just then, Dad drove into the yard with his bike tied onto the roof rack of Uncle Bill's car. Lizzie and Jack looked at each other - what sort of mood would he be in this time?

'Hello you two! What have you got there?' he asked as he came into the kitchen and put his arms around them. 'Oh strawberries! Some for jam and some to eat right now!' And with that, he took a handful and popped them in his mouth. 'Mmm, that's good!' he said, licking his lips. Jack and Lizzie grinned. This was more like the Dad they knew.

'There's another car coming,' said Mum, looking out of the window. 'It's Mr Rosen and he has all his family with him.'

Mr Rosen was the vet who looked after all the animals on the farm. He gave them injections to stop them catching diseases and medicine when they were sick. He even came to see them in the middle of the night if something was wrong.

Jack followed Dad into the yard. 'Hello Mr Rosen,' he called, running to the car.

'Hello, Jack,' said Mr Rosen. 'I'm afraid we've come to say goodbye.'

'When do you leave?' asked Dad.

'We're going to the harbour now. I really hate leaving. I don't know whether there'll be any vets left in Jersey.'

'This shouldn't be happening, it's not right,' said Dad, shaking his head.

'I know, I know,' sighed Mr Rosen. 'But I have to get my family as far away from the Nazis as I can. Here are my keys. Will you look after the surgery for me, John?'

'Of course I will, Matthew,' Dad replied.

'Well, goodbye,' said Mr Rosen. 'I hope we'll meet again when the war is over.'

'Goodbye and good luck my friend, keep safe,' said Dad, and they watched the car disappear into the distance.

'Come on, son, we have work to do. The cows need milking,' Dad said as he walked into the stable and picked up his bucket. He sat down on a small wooden three-legged stool ready to milk Bluebell, one of Jack's favourite cows. He squeezed her teats and milk squirted into the bucket and Jack sat on a bale of straw watching him thoughtfully.

'Does Mr Rosen have to go because he's English like Aunt May?' he asked.

'No, he's Jewish, Jack,' answered Dad.

'So the Germans don't like Jewish people either,' said Jack as he pulled pieces of straw out of the bale.

'No, they don't,' Dad said, looking up from his milking, 'and I really don't understand it at all.'

Jack was quiet again for a while. Even his Dad didn't understand, but he had one more question to ask.

'Dad, who are the Nazis? I thought it was the

Germans who were coming,' he asked.

'Well it's complicated. The Nazis are the people who rule Germany. Just like the men in the States of Jersey rule Jersey and the Members of Parliament in London rule England.'

'Are the Nazis German people?' asked Jack.

'Most of them are German,' Dad replied, 'but the man in charge comes from Austria and his name is Adolf Hitler. He's a very wicked man, Jack. He wants to rule the world and all the people who agree with him are called Nazis. Hitler started this war.' He looked at Jack's bewildered face and got up from his stool. 'Come here son,' he said, hugging him in his big strong arms. 'We'll get through it, don't you worry.'

Just then Mr Le Brun, their neighbour from Spring Farm and his son Richard, who was Jack's school friend, came into the stable. Richard was carrying a large cardboard box which he put down on the floor.

'What's in there?' asked Jack curiously.

'It's some food from our larder,' explained Richard. 'There's bread, sugar and...' Suddenly, before they could stop him, Scratch grabbed some bacon from the box and raced out into the yard.

'Scratch, bad dog!' shouted Jack, as he and Richard ran after him. Round and round the yard they went, but Scratch was determined not to give it back. Dad and Mr Le Brun stood at the stable door laughing.

'Let him have it, he deserves a treat,' called Dad.

'And we must go, Richard,' said Mr Le Brun, who turned to Dad and gave him the suitcase he was carrying. 'It's just some books and papers that we can't take with us. I'd be very grateful if you could look after it, John.'

'Yes, of course,' answered Dad.

'Are you going to England too?' Jack asked Richard. He nodded, then went to his father and took hold of his hand.

'It won't be for long,' said Mr Le Brun.

'Good luck my friend,' said Dad.

'Bye, Richard,' called Jack, feeling, very sad that his cousin and now his best friend from school would both be in England.

But a few hours later there was a knock at the door. It was Mr Le Brun coming back to collect his things. The boats were full; they would have to stay in Jersey.

That evening, as Jack and his family sat at the kitchen table eating their supper, they thought of all the people who had left.

'I hear that the baker's gone,' said Dad.

'And the dentist too,' said Poppa.

'That's good, I don't like going to see him!' said Lizzie with a laugh.

'And did you know that young Michael from the village has gone to join the Navy?' asked Dad.

'Yes, and I think quite a few other men are going to join the Army, Navy or even the RAF,' answered Poppa.

Mum dipped bread soldiers into a soft boiled egg and gave them to Thomas, who was sitting in his wooden high chair.

'The vicar and all his family have gone, I'll miss them so much,' she said sadly.

'Me too,' Maman whispered, trying not to cry. Jack and Lizzie listened quietly. Everything was changing and it felt very, very sad.

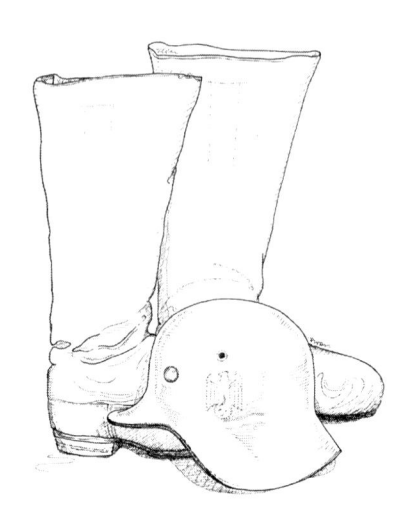

Chapter Four

They're Here!

By June 19th 1940, all the British soldiers had gone and there was no one left to defend Jersey. Everyone just had to wait; scared of what might happen next.

For ten days nothing happened. Jack and Lizzie were at home as all the schools were closed and Dad told the family that they had to carry on as normal. So he dug the potatoes in the field and Mum made some lovely crispy bread, but Jack just sat on the garden wall and sulked.

He didn't want to go fishing on his own, Lizzie

wouldn't play football with him and every day he had to go to Belle Vue to collect Scratch, who ran back to his old home. Jack missed Simon and was really fed up.

'What are you doing there?' asked Dad as he passed by.

'There's no one to play with,' moaned Jack.

'Well, there's plenty of work to be done. The animals can't look after themselves. If you collect some leaves to feed to the rabbits, then I'll come with you to Belle Vue and we can feed the pigs. Does that sound like a good plan?'

'Oh yes!' said Jack, jumping off the wall. He hurried off to look for dandelion leaves and clover and soon his basket was full. He fed the hungry rabbits that lived in two big hutches in the shed, then went to find Dad.

'I'm ready,' he called, running into the potato field.

'Good lad,' Dad replied. 'Come on, let's go.'

Jack grabbed Dad's hand and together they set off through the fields. They crossed the stream and started to climb the hill to the farm yard. Suddenly they heard the distant drone of engines. They searched the sky until they saw tiny grey dots appear from behind the clouds. The dots grew larger and turned into a formation of planes flying from the French coast. They got closer and closer, flew over the beach and seemed to be coming straight towards them.

"Lie down NOW!" Dad shouted, as he pushed Jack to the ground and threw himself on top of his son to protect him. Jack caught his breath and froze. The noise got louder as the planes came lower over their heads, but nothing happened and they disappeared into the distance.

Suddenly BOOM! BOOM! BOOM! Sounds from somewhere over the hill. Then another boom, so loud that they felt a pain in their ears and a rumbling feeling in their chests. Then silence. Neither of them moved and all Jack could hear was the thump of his father's heart.

'It's alright, son,' said Dad, as he stood up and pulled Jack to his feet. 'Are you hurt?'

'No Dad, but what happened?' replied Jack, brushing the grass off his knees. He felt a bit scared and shaky, as he waited for his father to reply.

'I think they've bombed the town. I hope no one was hurt.'

'Will they come back?'

'I don't know, Jack, but I'm sure that the Germans will land here very soon. There's absolutely nothing we can do to stop them, nothing at all,' answered Dad with a sigh. 'Well come on, we still have pigs to feed, I'm sure they won't have liked all that noise!' With that, he strode off towards the farm, lost in thought and looking very sad. Jack followed him and climbed into the pigsty, where the frightened pigs were grunting loudly. As he fed them, he felt very, very afraid.

Later that day when the family was getting ready to eat their meal, the telephone rang. It was Uncle Frank. He told them that German bomber planes had used machine guns to shoot at people and had also bombed the harbour. Ten people had been killed and many others injured.

'I thought you said they would land without bombing us,' wailed Lizzie.

'We really hoped they wouldn't attack. I think they're trying to frighten us so that we'll surrender,' answered Mum.

'Those Nazis!' Dad shouted, banging his fist on the table and making everyone jump. 'How dare they do this to us!' He stormed out of the kitchen, slammed the door and disappeared up the drive.

'It's alright, eat your supper,' Mum said, trying to keep everyone calm. But no one felt hungry now. Soon Jack and Lizzie went up the stairs to bed wondering what tomorrow would bring.

For three days they all tried to carry on as if nothing bad was happening. Then, early the next morning, they heard the planes again. They were so scared. Would the Germans drop bombs on them this time? Lizzie screamed and grabbed hold of Dad, who rushed into the dining room and lifted up a trapdoor leading to a tiny cellar below.

'Quick! Everyone go down into the cellar, we'll be safe there,' he shouted, as the sound of the planes grew louder. He helped Maman down the steep steps and the rest of the family followed. Thomas cried loudly, kicking his little legs; he didn't want to go into the dark, dark hole.

'John, fetch a candle and some matches,' Mum called as she tried to calm Thomas. A few minutes later the trapdoor was closed. By the flickering light of the candle, they could see each other's frightened faces as they waited to see what would happen next. But this time, there was no bombing at all. Instead, the Germans had dropped papers with messages written on them, telling everyone what they had to do. If they didn't obey then the island would be bombed again.

The messages said that a large white cross had to be painted on the middle of the Royal Square by the States building, and everyone was told to fly a white flag on their houses, offices and shops. This would be a sign that Jersey was surrendering. Then, in the afternoon, the Bailiff and other government officials had to go to the airport to meet the German Commandant and his soldiers.

Mum and Dad fixed an old white sheet onto their bedroom window and from the yard the family watched the planes as they flew over the farm. The roaring sounds of their engines made Jack cover his ears and Lizzie started to cry. They all knew that hundreds of soldiers would be landing at the airport. It was 1st July 1940 and the Germans had arrived.

The next day, Dad sat at the table drinking his cider and read the headline in local newspaper, the Evening Post. It said, "Orders of the Commandant of the German Forces in Occupation of the Island of Jersey", followed by orders that everyone had to obey. He wondered how he could keep his family safe with the German soldiers ruling the island. Mum looked at him and her three children as she stirred the stew that was bubbling away on the stove. She loved them all so much and would look after them whatever happened. Thomas began to cry; even he seemed to know that something strange was going on.

'It's alright, Thomas,' she said, as she picked him

up and kissed him. Lizzie and Jack watched in silence; they dared not speak in case Dad lost his temper again. After a while, Lizzie pulled on Jack's sleeve to get his attention.

'Let's go and see Maman,' she whispered. Jack nodded and they tiptoed out of the kitchen and ran across the yard.

They loved going to Maman and Poppa's little old cottage. It always felt safe and cosy with its three tiny windows, two small red chimneys and old wooden door that divided into two so that you could open the top half and leave the bottom half closed. In the spring, beautiful white roses grew over the door and honeysuckle climbed up the walls. In the daytime, Poppa's pigeons sat on the roof and cooed and, at night, the bats that lived in holes in the roof flew out to catch insects, then returned to feed their babies.

As they opened the door, they could hear the sound of the wireless in the kitchen and the news of the occupation of the Channel Islands was being announced. They peered round the corner and saw Maman sitting at the old oak table, sipping her cup of tea and Poppa sitting in his armchair by the fire, puffing on a cigarette. He was tapping his hand on the arm of the chair and shaking his head. His white hair flopped over his eyes and he pushed it back over his big bald patch and then threw his cigarette onto the fire.

'Poppa,' said Jack, expecting him to turn to him.

'Shhh! be quiet,' came the gruff reply. Maman looked up and smiled

'Come here, my lovelies,' she said, putting her arms out towards them then hugging them close. 'What a sad, sad time. It's a good thing I can look after you and you can look after me, don't you think?'

'Yes, Maman, it is,' said Lizzie giving her a big kiss.

'Now off you go, Poppa needs some peace and quiet,' Maman said. Lizzie and Jack crept out again and sat on the wall by the pigeon loft in the corner of the yard. Scratch came to find them and sat at their feet, but they didn't want to play. Suddenly Lizzie grabbed hold of Jack, let out a wail and burst into tears.

'What will happen to us now?' she cried.

'Shut up, Lizzie!' shouted Jack, pushing her away.

'But what are we going to do? What will the soldiers do to us?'

'I don't know, you silly girl. Leave me alone!' he yelled, jumping off the wall and running down the path towards the woods. 'Come on, Scratch' he called. Scratch bounded through the grass towards him and together they splashed through the stream and walked into the wood until they reached the old oak tree. Jack sat down on the soft moss, lent against the old gnarled tree trunk and held Scratch's face in his hands.

'Everyone's being really silly,' he said. 'Make sure that you don't start behaving like them, do you hear me?' Scratch wagged his tail and Jack felt that his doggie friend understood exactly what he meant.

He climbed into the branches of his tree and looked far into the distance. He thought of all the boys and girls in France who already knew what it was like to have German soldiers in their villages and towns and he wondered what was happening to them. He felt very scared. Normally he would have run to Mum and Dad for reassurance, but today he didn't want to go back home, so he took Scratch across Uncle Bill's field to the lane and walked towards the village. They passed his school and the empty baker's shop and soon reached the Parish Hall.

Suddenly, he stopped, grabbed Scratch's collar and stared. In front of the hall was a large black car and attached to its bonnet, fluttering in the breeze, was a small flag with a funny looking cross on it. As Jack watched, three men in uniform got out of the car. 'They're German soldiers and that must be their flag,' he thought to himself as he crouched down behind a low wall. Scratch growled, 'Shhh,' Jack whispered, pulling him down too.

Two of the soldiers, carrying rifles over their left shoulders, stood to attention, one on each side of the Parish Hall front door. Their uniforms were green with dark green collars and they wore long black boots and helmets that Jack thought looked rather like the pot in which mum cooked the stew. The third man's uniform was slightly different; he wore a cap and seemed to be the officer in charge. When the Parish Constable came out to meet them, he looked very stern. The officer spoke to him and he nodded sadly.

After a while the soldiers got back into the car and drove away, leaving the Constable standing on the doorstep. He put his head in his hands and sighed, then went back indoors looking very, very miserable.

Jack stood up. Now he had seen and heard the enemy. He turned and ran as fast as he could until he reached his home, where he burst into the kitchen, with Scratch following on behind.

'Dad, I've seen them!' he gasped. 'The Germans are in the village.'

'You're late. Sit down and eat your supper,' Dad said angrily, without even looking up at him.

'But Dad!'

'Do as you're told, Jack!' he ordered. Jack looked at Mum, then Lizzie, who just shrugged her shoulders but did not speak. He sat down but was so cross that he had a job to swallow the food Mum put in front of him.

As soon as he could, he left the table, took Scratch upstairs to his bedroom and shut the door.

'They won't even listen,' he said, as they both jumped onto his bed. 'They'll have a big shock in the morning when they see German soldiers in the village.' Jack lay down and thought about all he had seen and heard. He felt very small and alone. 'I'm glad you're here, Scratch,' he said, putting his arms around the collie dog. Scratch licked his face contentedly as they snuggled down together. 'We'll have to look after each other, won't we?' But Scratch didn't hear, he was fast asleep. Soon Jack was too, dreaming of soldiers with guns, wearing mum's cooking pots on their heads.

Chapter Five

Rules! Rules! Rules!

The Germans were the bosses now and there were Rules! Rules! Rules! Every day, written in the newspaper, there were more orders and notices telling them what to do and what would happen if they disobeyed. Sometimes the rules actually helped everyone in the island live and work together quite well. At other times they were not helpful at all.

Jack and his family settled into a strange routine, trying to remember all that they had been told. When it was dark, all the window had to be covered up so that no light would shine out through the glass. This was called the blackout and the Germans were very strict about it. Every night Dad went round the house and made sure that not even a speck of light shone out from the farmhouse.

Sometimes they couldn't switch on their lights as electricity was rationed, so Mum found all the old candles that were packed away in the attic and lit two when the children did their homework and when the family ate their supper. It was very difficult to read or play cards in such a dim light, so usually they all went to bed early and waited for daylight to come.

Everyone had to have an identity card with their name, age and a small picture of themselves pasted onto it. Soldiers could ask to see these at any time and there would be trouble if you did not have it with you.

As time went by, more and more goods were rationed so everyone had to have a ration card. Mum read the Evening Post every day to find out what she could buy and sometimes there would be some sugar, coffee or another treat. Then she took the family's ration cards to the village shop and the shopkeeper recorded what she bought to make sure that she had no more than her fair share.

The family liked to sit round their wireless set and

listen to the news from England, but soon the Germans ordered that all wirelesses had to be handed in to them. Dad gave them the big wireless, but Poppa kept his tiny one and hid it in the pigeon loft where he would sit and listen very quietly while Maman kept guard. They really wanted to know what was happening in the rest of the world, but this was a very dangerous thing to do, as if they were caught, they would be sent to prison.

Most of the time the beaches were out of bounds and barbed wire fences were put up to stop anyone getting to the sea and escaping to England by boat.

'You must stay away from the beach,' said Dad sternly. 'The Germans have planted landmines in the sand ready to explode if anyone treads on them.' Jack felt very upset that he couldn't go fishing, play in the rock pools, or take Scratch for walks by the sea.

One particular rule made Dad very cross indeed. Nearly everyone, except for doctors and a few other important people, had to give their cars and lorries to the Germans.

'This is ridiculous! How can we run the farm without our lorry?' Dad asked Poppa.

'We never had lorries in my day!' answered Poppa. 'I'm sure we can mend the old van and cart that are in the barn.'

'Yes, make do and mend, there's always a way!' said Maman with a smile.

'You're right, we have to make the best of it,' said Dad. 'Come on, let's get them out and see what we can do.'

There were cobwebs everywhere! The cart was full of straw and the van piled high with old boxes. As Jack helped Dad clean up the cart, he thought of Simon and all the games they used to play. They would pretend to be Roman warriors invading England, and the cart, with its two big wheels and wooden seat at the front, was their chariot. The van, which was much bigger, was their camp.

'And now we've been invaded just like the people long ago,' he thought with a sigh, sitting down on a bale of straw and watching as Poppa and Dad mended, painted and polished.

'Well, Jack, I think this cart is as good as new, don't you?' asked Dad, brushing the cobwebs out of his hair. 'Come on; help me take it out into the yard.' Jack took hold of one of the long poles onto which the horses could be harnessed and together they pulled it out into the sunshine for everyone to see.

'This brings back many happy memories,' said Maman. 'Do you think Chestnut and Robin will remember how to pull it?'

'It will take them a while, but I'm sure they'll be fine,' said Poppa. 'Tomorrow we'll mend the van, then we can see how well they can do.'

After a bit of practice, the horses learnt how to pull the small cart and huge van and the family got used to life without having a lorry on their farm.

There was one rule that nobody liked at all! At night time everyone had to stay inside their houses. This was called the curfew. If someone was found outside, they could be arrested and taken to the prison in the town. Poppa soon found out exactly what would happen if you disobeyed this rule.

One dark night, after he had checked that his pigeons were settled in the pigeon loft and Maman had put the rabbits in their hutches and the chickens safely in the henhouse, they sat by the fire in their little cottage. They were tired after a busy day's work and Poppa soon fell asleep and began to snore. Maman was knitting by candlelight when suddenly she heard a loud mooing sound coming from the meadow. At first, she didn't take much notice, but the mooing went on and on.

'There's something wrong with that cow,' she thought. 'She sounds very unhappy.' She prodded

Poppa with her knitting needle, making him jump.

'What's up! What did you do that for?' he grumbled.

'Listen, there's a cow in trouble.' she replied. Poppa heard it too.

'I think it could be Dewdrop,' he said. 'She should be having her calf soon, maybe she needs my help.'

'You can't go out there now, it's after curfew,' said Maman. Poppa took no notice.

'There she goes again!' he said. 'I'm sure it's Dewdrop. If she can't manage to give birth to her calf by herself, they could both die. I'm going out'

'No! Please don't go! You might get caught,' pleaded Maman.

'I'll be fine. You know I can't leave a cow in trouble,' answered Poppa as he put on his coat and picked up his lamp with its candle fixed inside.

'You can't take a lamp outside, the Germans in the village might see the light and come to investigate. If they find you, you'll be arrested,' said Maman, who was very worried indeed.

'Don't worry,' said Poppa. He blew out the candles in the house so that light would not shine out when he opened the door and stepped into the darkness.

Everything was quiet except for the moo, moo,

mooing of Dewdrop. 'I wish the moon was shining, I really can't see where I'm going,' Poppa said to himself. 'I'll have to light the lamp.' As he lit the candle, he put his hands round the lamp so that only a tiny beam shone through his fingers showing him the way. He carefully and quietly walked into the meadow and found Dewdrop lying on the grass, looking very sorry for herself.

'Well, Dewdrop, what's wrong with you?' he said, patting her back. 'Your calf has got a bit stuck hasn't it? Let's see if I can help.' Poppa put the light down on the grass and got to work. He loved his cows and soon forgot about the curfew as he helped Dewdrop give birth to her beautiful little calf.

'There you are, well done old girl,' he said, as the calf took a big breath and tried to stand up. Poppa guided it to its mother's teats and it began to drink the warm milk. He sat watching them, feeling very happy that there was now a new little calf on the farm. But as he turned to go back to the cottage, he heard heavy footsteps crunching on the gravel path.

'Oh no! The soldiers must have seen my light,' he thought, blowing out the candle and standing very still. 'Surely they'll understand that my cow needed me.'

'Come out now,' called a voice with a German

accent. 'We know you are there. Come out with your hands above your head or we'll shoot.'

Poppa had no choice. 'I'm coming,' he replied.

Just then, the moon came out from behind the clouds and Poppa could see two soldiers coming towards him. One pointed his gun at him and the other roughly grabbed him by the shoulder.

'You know the law. No one can be outside after curfew. What were you doing?'

'My cow was calving and needed my help,' said Poppa. 'I haven't been out for long.'

'That is no excuse,' said the soldier. 'The rule is there to be obeyed.'

'But she might have died, can't you see how important it was for me to be here?' answered Poppa.

'Do not make excuses. You must come with us. You broke the law and you must be punished,' said the soldier with the gun.

'My wife will be worried. Please let me tell her what has happened,' pleaded Poppa.

'You broke the law and you must be punished,' the soldier said again, prodding him in the back and marching him off up the drive. Poppa was really afraid now. He didn't know what they would do with him next.

Maman had heard the noise in the yard and realised that Poppa had been taken away. She wanted to tell John and Jane, but was scared to go outside and across to their door. She sat by the fire and waited and waited, but he did not come back. The fire went out but she didn't move. Would he be kept in prison? She did not know.

The next morning, as soon as it was light, Maman opened the door and peered outside. She hadn't slept at all and looked very, very tired. For a while she just sat on the wall by the pigeon loft trying to pluck up the courage to tell the family the bad news. Then, in the distance, she saw someone walking slowly towards her. It was Poppa! He was back! She laughed and rushed up the drive towards him, flinging her arms round his neck.

'Oh my dear, thank goodness you're safe. I thought I might never see you again, you silly old man.'

Poppa hugged her tight. 'That was a worrying night I must say!' he said. 'They threw me in a cell and I thought I might be staying there, but I was let off with a warning and told never to go out after curfew again.'

'I hope you've learnt your lesson!' said Maman.

'Well maybe. But you know, if my cows are in trouble,

I'll probably do it all over again.'

Maman shook her head. 'Yes, you probably will.'

'We don't need to tell the family, do we?' asked Poppa.

'No!' laughed Maman. 'It's best that they never know about your little adventure!'

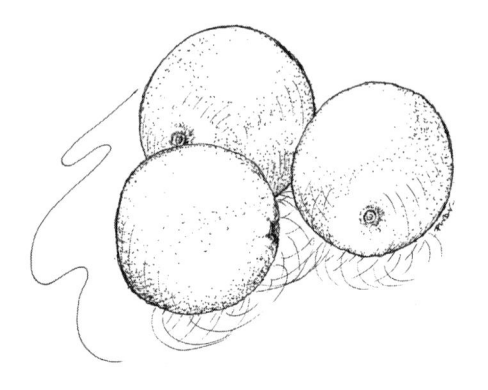

Chapter 6

A Trip To Town

The war went on and on and nobody knew when it would end. They longed for the day when they would be free again. Christmas came and even though many people had thought that the war would be over by then, the Germans were still occupying the Channel Islands.

Throughout the spring and summer Dad and Poppa worked in the fields, milked the cows, fed the pigs and took the vegetables to the market in the town. Mum cooked and cleaned and Maman looked after the turkeys that lived in the meadow, mended the children's clothes, and helped Mum in the kitchen. Lizzie and Jack looked after the chickens and rabbits and helped groom the horses. Everyone worked hard and they were very tired, but they tried to make the best of life and enjoy whatever they could.

Now it was winter again and on one cold windy day, Lizzie and Jack were very bored and grumpy. Lizzie wanted to draw a picture, but she had run out of paper and Jack wanted to paint his toy soldiers, but he had run out of paint. Only little Thomas seemed content as he pushed his little wooden tractor across the floor.

'Mum, have you got some paper I can use?' asked Lizzie pleadingly. 'I haven't any left at all, not even a tiny scrap!'

'Sorry, Lizzie, there's absolutely nothing for you to draw on,' Mum replied, looking up from her sewing. She felt sorry for her children and wished she could give them more. Then she had an idea. She stood up, took off her pinafore, hung it on the peg by the door and went out of the room.

Lizzie wondered what she was going to do as she hardly ever took off her pinafore (except on special occasions like going to church on Sundays, or when visitors came for tea). Soon she reappeared carrying her hat and coat.

'Come on you two, get your coats and scarves, let's go into town together as a special treat. Maman can look after Thomas and we'll go by bus and have a fun day out,' she said, laughing at her children's excited faces. 'We'll try to find paper, paint and some new shoes for you, Jack. What do you think?'

'Yes, yes!' shouted Jack, jumping up and down. He wanted paint and he really needed shoes. He had been wearing the same pair since before the war began nearly two years ago and as his feet had grown, his shoes were much too tight. They had huge holes in them too and even though Mum put cardboard inside them, his socks got very soggy in the rain.

'Can we visit Uncle Bill and Aunt Emily?' he asked, hoping his cousin Charles would be at home too and would have a game of football.

'Of course we can! And I know it's forbidden, but I think I'll take them some eggs,' Mum replied.

'And some strawberry jam?' asked Lizzie.

'That's a good idea. We'll take some homemade bread too, then we can stay for tea.'

'We're going into town! We're going on the charcoal bus to town,' sang Jack, doing a little dance round and round the table.

'Shut up, Jack!' laughed Lizzie.

Mum fetched the eggs, jam and bread and hid them at the bottom of her basket. 'I'll cover all this with a cloth so that the soldiers won't see what I've got in here,' she said. 'Are you ready? Good, it's time to go!'

Soon they were at the bus stop waiting for the old charcoal bus. It stopped and they climbed on board and set off for St Helier. Lizzie and Jack hardly ever went further than the village, so this was a real adventure.

'It feels funny to be driving on the wrong side of the road,' said Lizzie.

'That's another of the silly new rules we have to obey,' answered the bus conductor, who had overheard what she was saying. 'We're driving on the right now, like they do in Germany.'

They drove past the Parish Hall and Jack remembered the first time that he had seen the soldiers all those months ago. They passed empty houses with overgrown gardens, other homes with vegetable patches where there had been lawns and some that had been taken over by the Germans as homes for their soldiers. They saw tanks, some huge grey guns and soldiers with rifles who stood to attention and watched them pass by.

'Boys and girls, it's time to get off and walk,' called the conductor, as they reached the bottom of a steep hill. 'My old bus hasn't enough power to climb this hill with everyone on board.'

The children jumped down and ran as fast as they could to beat the bus to the top of the hill. It was great fun.

Soon they arrived at St Helier and Mum, Lizzie and Jack got off the bus and walked down the street. Jack felt as if he had come to an alien world. Some shops were boarded up, others were open (although their windows were almost bare or displayed only second-hand goods) and there were hardly any shoppers at all. Everywhere he looked there were groups of soldiers either standing to attention, or laughing and joking together. He stopped and looked at a flag with a swastika on it that was flying from the Town Hall.

'That's Hitler flag and I hate it and I really hate him too!' he said to himself, folding his arms and frowning. 'It's his fault that Simon has gone to England and all the soldiers are here.'

'Jack, don't even look at it,' said Mum. 'Come on now, let's go to the shoe shop.' But that didn't make Jack feel any better. All they could find were bootlaces for Dad. He was very disappointed.

'But I really need some shoes now,' he said, looking pleadingly at the shop keeper, who just shrugged his shoulders.

'I'm sorry, lad, we hope to receive some leather from France soon, then the cobbler will make some shoes for us to sell,' he replied. 'Some people are repairing their shoes with old car tyres, or making clogs out of wood, you know.' Jack didn't like that idea at all!

'Well, we'll have to give up shoe shopping for now', said Mum. 'Let's head for the market, I've heard that there are some walnuts for sale.'

When they arrived, they stopped and stared at what they saw.

'There's hardly anything here!' Lizzie exclaimed, looking at the empty fish stalls and the butchers with only a few rabbits and chickens on display.

'Look at the greengrocers, Mum,' said Jack. 'All they've got are apples, onions, potatoes and a few dried beans.'

'Oh dear, the market used to be such a colourful place, full of flowers and every kind of fruit and vegetable,' Mum replied sadly.

'I'd like to eat an orange right now!' said Lizzie, licking her lips and trying to remember what it tasted like.

'Well, Lizzie, look! You won't have to wait very long, there's a stall with a basket full of them.' Lizzie picked up an orange and sniffed it.

'Umm,' she said. 'Please can I have it, Mum?'

'They came from Spain,' explained the stallholder. 'There is one for each child, but I'm sorry, none for you,' he said, looking at Mum. So Mum bought three oranges and some walnuts and put them into her basket.

'Thomas has never eaten an orange, he'll probably put the whole thing in his mouth, peel and all!' she said laughingly. 'There'll be lots of new things for him to try when the war is over.'

'Everyone looks so thin and tired,' said Lizzie, as they walked down the street.

'The town people are very hungry. They can't grow food for themselves like we can. We're very lucky to live on a farm,' Mum replied. Lizzie and Jack agreed that they were very lucky indeed.

They hurried on to Uncle Frank's shop on the corner by the park. The shop was called 'The Parade Hardware Store' and the name was written on a sign swinging in the breeze above the door. The shop had two large windows with tape criss-crossed over them, so that they would not shatter if there was an explosion and a green door with a sign saying 'Welcome'.

As Jack opened the door, a little bell rang and Uncle

Frank looked up and smiled.

'What a surprise! Come in, come in,' he said. 'Emily, come and see who's here.'

Aunt Emily came out from their sitting room behind the shop and gasped, putting her hand over her mouth.

'Have you got news?' she asked.

'News?' replied Mum, who didn't know what she meant.

'From Bill, May and the children. Are they alright?'

'Oh Emily,' said Mum, giving her a hug. 'I'm sure they're fine in Manchester, but I'm sorry we haven't heard from them. We've just come to visit.'

'Oh I see. I just thought you might have news,' said Aunt Emily with a smile. 'It's so good to see you. Come into the sitting room, Jane; then we can have a good chat.' With that, she took mum by the arm and off they went.

Jack looked around. It didn't look like Uncle Frank's shop at all. Before the occupation he would spend hours rummaging through the shelves that were filled with everything you could ever need. Now there were a few saucepans, a piece of garden hose, some balls of string, nails, hooks, some boxes of matches and a few other bit and pieces scattered over dusty shelves, but that was all. He wasn't even sure that there would be any paint for his soldiers.

Uncle Frank watched him as he looked up and down the shelves. 'What is it you want, Jack?' he asked.

'I need some paint for my toy soldiers, they're chipped and dirty,' answered Jack.

'Sorry, I haven't any paint at all, supplies are really running low,' explained Uncle Frank shaking his head. 'Occasionally, ships come from France bringing goods for us to sell, but it's very difficult to find the things we need. Tell me, what would Maman say about these soldiers of yours?'

Jack grinned. 'She'd say, "make do and mend, there's always a way!"'

'That's right, Jack,' laughed Uncle Frank. 'There's always a way!'

'I'll clean them up, they'll be ok,' he said.

'Good lad,' Uncle Frank replied.

'Where's Charles?' asked Lizzie, who had been waiting patiently to speak to her uncle.

'He's gone to the park. Why don't you two go and join him,' answered Uncle Frank. 'Be careful, don't talk to the soldiers and come straight back if you can't find him.'

'We will,' Jack replied. He loved being with his older

cousin, but since the war began they hadn't seen him very often. Lizzie and Jack ran to the park, where they found Charles sitting on a bench, chewing a blade of grass and looking rather sad.

'Hello, Charles,' said Lizzie, sitting down beside him.

'Hello you two!' said Charles. 'What are you doing here?'

'We came to buy some shoes for Jack, but there's none in the shops,' she replied. 'What's wrong with you? You don't look very happy.'

'Well I'm not!' Charles said. 'There's nothing to do. We can't go to the harbour or the beach, and we're not even allowed to play football any more. Now Mum and Dad won't let me go off on my bike with my friends because they say we'll get up to mischief and end up in trouble. It's really, really boring stuck in the shop with them.' He spat out the grass and frowned.

'We'll all be back at school soon and then you can see your friends,' said Jack.

'I won't be going back. I had to leave at the end of last term because I'm fifteen now.'

'What are you going to do?' asked Lizzie.

'I don't know. We don't have enough customers in the shop for me to be able to work with Dad.' Jack and Lizzie felt very sorry for their cousin and rather embarrassed that they had so much and he had so little. Jack quickly changed the subject.

'We're going to stay at your house for tea. Let's go back to the shop,' he said.

'There's not much to eat. We even have to go to the communal kitchen now,' said Charles.

'What's a communal kitchen?' asked Lizzie.

'Well, Mum puts a few potatoes, parsnips or carrots in a baking tray, covers them with water and takes them to a kitchen on the other side of town. They cook it for us there.'

'Why don't you do it at home like we do?' asked Lizzie.

'We don't have any wood or coal to light our stove. Nobody does. You're really lucky to live on a farm, you know,' answered Charles, angrily. 'It's not much fun living in the town.'

'Mum has brought you some eggs, bread and strawberry jam,' said Jack, hoping that this would cheer him up.

'Did you say strawberry jam? I haven't had jam for ages.'

'Yes, we made it ourselves! Come on,' Lizzie replied. So they all headed back to the shop for tea.

Everyone sat round the table enjoying boiled eggs and toast, bread and jam and a kind of tea made from blackberry leaves. It was the best meal the town family had had for a long time.

'Aunt Jane and I have been talking about what you could do now that you've left school, Charles,' said Uncle Frank. 'You know that we haven't got enough work for you in the shop, and we don't want the Germans making you work for them, so how about staying on the farm and helping Uncle John?'

Charles looked at his father in surprise. 'Really, Dad! Do you really mean that I can go to work on the farm?' he asked in amazement.

Uncle Frank laughed 'Of course I really mean it!' he said, feeling very relieved that Charles was so enthusiastic.

'So you'd like to come, would you?' asked his aunt.

'Oh yes please! Thank you, Aunt Jane, it would be fun!' he replied, grinning from ear to ear.

'Fun and a lot of hard work too!' she said laughingly.

'Do you mind if I go, Mum?' Charles asked. Aunt Emily looked at her son's excited face.

'I really don't want you to go, but I know it will be the best thing for you,' she replied.

'Thanks Mum. When can I start?'

'We'll collect your things together and you can go on the bus on Monday. How about that?' she answered with a smile.

'You'll be able to help us with our chores!' said Lizzie.

'And play football with me in the field!' said Jack.

Charles laughed and slapped Jack on the back. 'I can't wait!' he exclaimed. Just then the big clock above the fireplace struck five.

'We have to go now if we're to catch the last bus before curfew,' said Mum. 'Come on you two.'

'Thank you for our splendid tea,' said Aunt Emily.

'I'm so pleased we had something special to bring you,' Mum replied, as they put on their coats and went to the door.

'Wait a minute, Lizzie, I've got something for you,' said Uncle Frank, giving her a parcel wrapped in an old piece of cloth. Inside she found a tiny notebook. It wasn't new, but had many clean pages for her to use.

'Oh thank you, Uncle,' she exclaimed, giving him a big kiss.

'We'll see you very soon, Charles,' said Mum, taking hold of her children's hands. 'Goodbye everyone.'

'Dad will be pleased to have some help on the farm.

And I think you two will enjoy Charles' company, won't you?' she asked, as they waited for the bus. They grinned. Yes, they certainly would!

It had been a good day, but now they were longing to get home to eat their very special orange treat!

Chapter Seven

Hide That Pig!

One sunny spring morning, when Jack and Lizzie were picking dandelion leaves and clover to feed the rabbits, Richard rode past on his old rusty bike. He was going so fast that he nearly ran into Jack, who jumped onto the hedge to get out of the way.

'Watch out!' Jack shouted, but Richard took no notice and didn't stop until he reached the yard where Dad was grooming the horses. He spoke to Dad, then turned around and pedalled towards Jack again.

'You'd better go back home,' he called, as he raced

past. 'Bye, Jack, bye, Lizzie!'

'I wonder what's going on?' said Lizzie. 'Come on, let's find out.' They picked up their bundles of rabbit food and raced back into the yard.

Dad had gone into the pigsty and he soon reappeared carrying a tiny squealing piglet under his arm, wrapped in an old blanket.

'Quick! Find Charles!' he said. 'The German inspectors are searching the farms again and they're counting and tattooing the piglets.' Jack raced down to the meadow and returned with Charles.

'Richard came to tell us that the soldiers are inspecting the farms, they're at Spring Farm now,' Dad explained. 'We've got one more piglet than we should have, so they'll take it away if they find it and I could be in a lot of trouble.' Charles took the squealing piglet from him and tucked it under his arm.

'Ok, Charles, you've done this before so you know what to do. Stay in the woods until you are sure the inspectors have left Spring Farm, then take the piglet to Mrs Le Brun.'

'I'll be careful, Uncle John,' Charles replied as he turned to go.

'Can I go too?' asked Jack.

'Yes, but do as Charles says. Once the inspector has

counted the other piglets and has left the farm, I'll come to get you.'

Charles had been living with the family for six months and he loved working on the farm. He really enjoyed playing football and cricket with Jack, but he felt rather cross that Jack was allowed to go with him to hide the pig.

'You heard what Uncle John said, do exactly what I say,' he told Jack as they ran through the meadow.

'Ok, I will,' Jack replied. Once they were well hidden amongst the trees, they slowed down, hoping that the frightened little piglet would stay quiet. All of a sudden, it squealed and its head popped out from under the blanket. Then it wriggled and wriggled, fell out of Charles' arms and ran away as fast as it could.

'Quick, after it!' whispered Charles. The two boys chased after the squealing piglet as it ran round and round the trees, through the undergrowth, then disappeared into the brambles.

'You're smaller than me, you can get through there,' said Charles, giving Jack the blanket and pushing him into the brambles.

'Ouch, ouch, stop it!' Jack exclaimed.

'Be quiet, Jack, just get the piglet,' said Charles.

'But the thorns are scratching me!'

'Just get that pig!!' said Charles, giving him another push.

'It's alright for you, you're wearing long trousers but I'm just wearing shorts,' Jack replied, feeling very annoyed.

'Shorts are for little boys who have to obey me!' answered Charles angrily. 'Hurry up. We have to get the piglet now!'

'I wish I'd stayed at home!' said Jack, pulling some thorns off his jumper.

'I wish you'd stayed at home too!' replied Charles.

The boys were so cross with each other that they hadn't noticed that the piglet had stopped. Then, Jack heard a little grunt and he crept forward. There it was, sniffing the ground under the blackberry bush not far ahead. Jack threw the blanket over its head and soon the squealing, kicking piglet was wrapped up tightly again.

'Got you!' he said, putting one hand over its snout so that it couldn't make any more noise. He backed his way out of the bushes and handed the pig to Charles, glaring at him for being so mean, then he marched off towards the farm, with Charles following on behind. Mrs Le Brun saw them coming and opened the door.

'Come in, come in, I've been expecting you. The

inspector has counted our pigs so we won't be bothered again,' she said. They followed her into the kitchen and Charles put the piglet on the floor.

'Oh Jack, look at your legs, what happened?' asked Mrs Le Brun, looking quite concerned.

'Just a few scratches,' he replied crossly. Mrs Le Brun could see that the boys were not very happy.

'Would you like a glass of milk?' she asked, 'I might be able to find a piece of cake too; you'll need to stay here for a while.'

'Yes please,' they both replied. Just then, Richard rushed into the kitchen.

'Oh good, you got here! Where's the pig?' he asked.

'There, look,' answered Jack, pointing at the piglet as he sniffed the cat and the cat spat at the piglet, then they curled up together in front of the fire and fell fast asleep.

'Thanks for coming to warn us, Richard,' said Charles. 'The inspectors must be at our farm by now,' said Charles. Richard grinned.

'It was a very bumpy ride, the tyres for my bike are broken so Dad has put pieces of hose pipe around the wheels instead,' he said.

'You're very lucky to have a bike that works,' said his mum. Everyone went quiet and the only sound was the crackling fire and the occasional snort from the piglet. As Jack munched his delicious cake, he wondered what was happening back at the farm.

'Do you think they're alright?' he asked putting his empty glass on the table and wiping his hand across his mouth.

'I'm sure they are, they know what to do,' said Mrs Le Brun reassuringly.

Back at the farm, everyone did know what to do because they had practised many times. Dad carried Thomas into the yard as it was his job to keep him safe in his arms until the inspector had left. Lizzie and Mum had to check that everything was in place in the dining room. This was a very important job as the cellar under its floor had a secret. It was the perfect hiding place for all their valuable possessions and the things Aunt May, Uncle Bill and Mr Rosen had given them for safe keeping. There were also barrels of potatoes, three sacks of wheat and a pile of turnips hidden away from the inspectors. Mum covered the trapdoor with an old red carpet and Lizzie helped her push a large bookcase on top of it, so that no one would know that it was there.

'Everything looks fine don't you think, Lizzie? I'm sure they'll never realise that there's a cellar under here,' she said, closing the dining room door. 'Make sure you don't look in this direction, or the inspector might get suspicious and wonder what you are looking at.'

'I'll be careful,' Lizzie replied. 'I'll get my book and pretend to read.' She could hear Poppa huffing and puffing as he climbed up the stairs to the attic, and wondered why he needed to go up there.

'What's he doing?' she asked Mum.

'Just making sure everything is in order,' Mum replied. She couldn't tell her that Poppa had moved his wireless from the pigeon loft to the attic and needed to check that it was well hidden behind the loose bricks in the wall. This was a much safer hiding place, and when the children were at school, he listened to the news from London.

It was Maman's job to keep the inspector out of the house until Poppa came back downstairs. She moved her chair onto the doorstep, sat down with an old cardigan of Mum's and began to unravel it, ready to knit up again into a jumper for Lizzie.

Soon, they heard Scratch bark and a car drove into the yard.

'Come here,' called Dad, as Scratch ran around the car. Scratch ran to Dad and sat beside him. 'Good boy, now stay.' Dad greeted the inspector and a soldier as they got out of the car.

'All stay here,' ordered the inspector, who then left the soldier to guard them while he went off to count the animals and inspect the crops. The family waited silently, knowing that soon he would come into the house. After a while, the inspector arrived at the kitchen door. He was stern and did not speak as he waited for Maman to get out of her chair. She slowly picked up the tangled wool and only when she was sure that Poppa had come back in the kitchen, did she move out of the way.

Dad told Thomas that he had to be very quiet and gave him an apple to munch; Mum prayed that the inspector wouldn't find the wireless or the cellar; Lizzie stared at her book and Poppa puffed on his cigarette, feeling angry that the enemy was on his farm.

The inspector disappeared upstairs and they could hear his heavy footsteps as he went into each bedroom, then climbed up to the attic. They held their breath and listened. Would he find Poppa's hiding place? Soon they heard the footsteps again and the inspector came down and went into the dining room. They heard him open drawers and move books on the old oak bookcase. He seemed to stop, maybe he'd found the trap door!

Lizzie put her hand over her mouth to stop the cry that was welling up inside her and Mum quietly went over to her daughter and stroked her long brown hair.

'Shhh, it's alright,' she whispered.

Eventually the inspector returned to the kitchen carrying a photo of the family that had been taken just before the war began.

'Everything seems to be in order,' he said. Then he studied the photo carefully. 'You have a lovely family.'

'Yes, thank you,' replied Mum politely.

'I have a young son. Look, here's a picture of him,' he said, handing Mum a crumpled picture of a baby and his smiling mother. 'He was born just before the war began.'

'He's very handsome. Are your wife and little boy well?'

'I haven't heard from them for months now. I hope they are alright. So many bad things are happening to us all,' he replied, shaking his head and kissing the photo. He sighed and put it back in his pocket. 'We have finished here. Goodbye.'

The family watched as he got into his car and disappeared up the drive, with Scratch barking and chasing after it.

'You know, I feel sorry for him. He's a family man

too,' said Mum.

'Yes, there must be many soldiers here in Jersey who didn't want to join the army. They had no choice at all,' answered Dad. Then they all breathed a big sigh of relief and began to laugh.

'Well, thank goodness that's over!' said Maman.

'Yes, our plan worked!' said Dad, giving his mother a hug. 'We really are a good team, don't you think?' And they all laughed again.

'Time for a cup of nettle tea and a piece of bread and jam to celebrate,' said Mum.

'That sounds perfect!' answered Dad. 'After that, I'll collect Charles and Jack, and the piglet too, of course!'

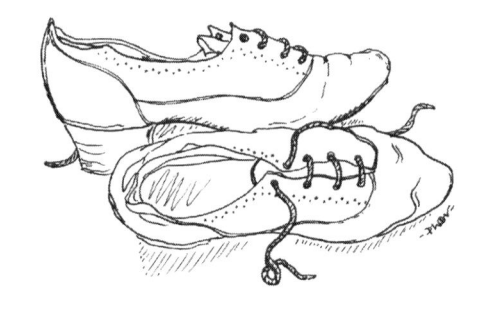

Chapter Eight

Life At School

Jack and Lizzie had to walk to school in the pouring rain and Jack was in a very bad mood. There was a big problem   his shoes!

'I won't wear them, I won't; you can't make me,' he shouted, as he ran through the kitchen, out into the yard and into the stable where Chestnut and Robin were happily munching hay.

'Jack,' called his father sternly. 'Come back now!' Jack didn't move. 'You have three choices. You can wear your old shoes to school, but you keep grumbling that they're too tight and full of holes. You can wear Maman's lace-up shoes or you can go to school in your socks! Just make sure that I see you walking up the drive in five minutes time.'

Jack felt very, very angry and threw himself down in the hay. All three choices were horrid! His toes hurt in his own shoes and it was too cold to go without any at all, but how could he possibly wear a pair of brown lace ups with heels belonging to his granny! Everyone would laugh at him – he was sure they would.

Just then, the stable door opened and Mum walked in.

'Come on, Jack. Let's talk about this shall we?' Jack looked up at his mother's kind face. 'I know it's hard, but it's the same for everyone. You know that some people are wearing clogs made of wood or shoes mended with old car tyres. There are some boys and girls who have to stay at home in wet cold weather as they don't have any shoes at all. Come on, it's not that bad.'

'But my friends will laugh at me, I know they will,' he whined, twisting bits of hay round and round his fingers.

Mum took hold of his hand. 'Listen Jack, you know what Maman always says – "make do and mend, there's always a way!" Lizzie has to go to school wearing a coat made out of the curtains we found in the attic. You told me yourself that Richard has a jumper knitted with wool from his Aunties' shawl.' Jack looked at her and nodded. 'Well, this is just the same. We all have to wear things we don't really like. No one has lovely new clothes now.'

'But they're lady's shoes,' he said, still not convinced.

'Yes, but they're warm and will keep your feet dry,' Mum replied.

He thought for a moment. He hadn't laughed when James in his class wore a coat belonging to his dad that went all the way down to his feet. Maybe he was quite lucky to have some strong warm shoes to wear for the winter.

'Alright, but if they make fun of me, I won't wear them again!' he said quietly.

'Good lad, off you go then or you'll have your father after you,' said Mum, ruffling his hair. He went back indoors and put on the shoes. He felt very embarrassed. A ten year old boy wearing women's shoes - this was dreadful!

As he walked up the drive he saw Charles, who was chopping wood in the field.

'Bye, Jack,' called out Charles, looking up as he passed by. Jack glared at him.

'Don't you dare say anything!' he shouted, angrily kicking the stones as hard as he could.

'What's wrong with you?' Charles asked in surprise. But Jack took no notice and continued on his way.

Soon he reached the school playground and he stood watching his friends as they ran around playing catch, or sat on the ground with their marbles. He was really surprised when nobody even noticed what he was wearing on his feet and he realised that all the children looked rather odd! Everyone was wearing something that would have embarrassed them before the occupation.

When the bell rang, Jack forgot about his shoes and lined up in the playground, ready for the day.

'Good morning, everyone,' said Mr Richardson, the headmaster, as he stood on the steps in front of them.

'Good morning sir,' they all replied.

'I have some very sad news for you today.' The children looked at each other wondering what he would say.

'I'm sorry to have to tell you that the Germans have deported Mr and Mrs Taylor and their family to Germany because they are English. I will teach Mr

Taylor's class.' There were gasps and the children began to talk to each other, shocked by what they had heard.

'Quiet please! Go to your classrooms now, thank you,' he said and he turned and disappeared inside.

Jack and the rest of his class marched indoors where Mrs Gray, their teacher, was waiting for them. They stood behind their chairs in silence, aware that there had been eleven children in their class and now there were only ten. Caroline Taylor had gone.

Mrs Gray smiled kindly at the shocked children.

'Good morning, class,' she said, as she stood behind her desk.

'Good morning, Mrs Gray,' came the reply.

'Sit down please. This is a sad day for us isn't it children? We will all miss Caroline very much and I really hope the family come back to us soon, but we have to carry on, work hard and do our best at this difficult time, don't you agree?' she asked gently.

'Yes, Mrs Gray,' the class replied. They loved and trusted their teacher and although she was strict, they knew that she would help and care for them while they were in school. They all thought the name Mrs Gray suited her very well. She had grey hair tied up in a little bun and she always wore a long black skirt and a white blouse fastened up to her chin with a pretty pink brooch. Her grey jacket had big black patches sewn onto the elbows and when she was cold, she put a dark grey shawl over her shoulders. She had taught many of their parents so she was quite old, but as so many teachers had evacuated to England just before the occupation began, she had come back to help at the school.

'Let's have a quick look behind the picture to cheer ourselves up shall we?' she suggested. The children nodded and grinned. They knew exactly what they would be doing next.

In the classroom with its brown floor, brown walls, brown desks and brown chairs, there were only two bits of colour. One was a red chart with the times tables on it and the other, a large picture of a ship with all its sails billowing in the wind as it sailed across the rough sea. Below the picture was part of a poem called Sea Fever. The children had learned to recite it and now they said it together, imagining life on the ocean waves.

'I must go down to the seas again, to the lonely sea and the sky,

And all I ask is a tall ship and a star to steer her by.'

But the picture and poem had a secret; a secret that

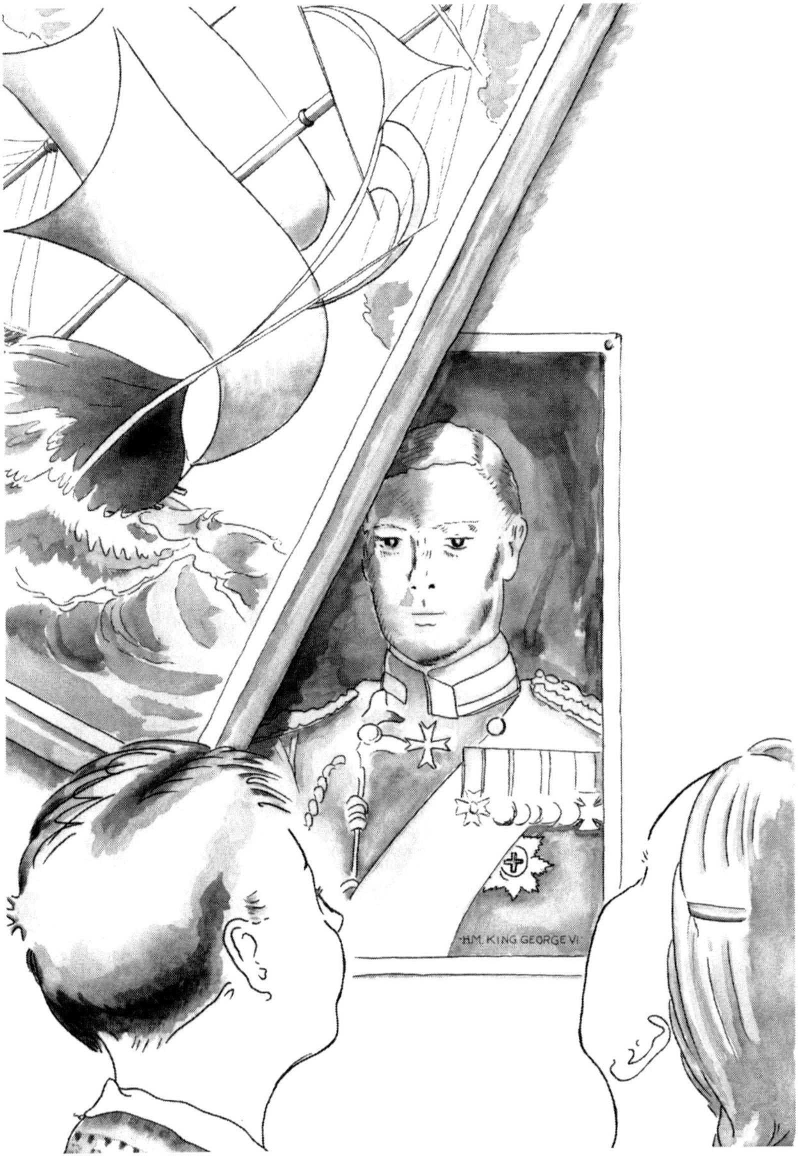
H.M. KING GEORGE VI

only Mrs Gray and the children knew. Behind that picture was a small photograph of King George VI, the King of England. Mrs Gray checked that no German soldiers were outside the door or windows and carefully removed the sailing ship.

'This is your King,' she said, pointing to the picture. 'We are British, never forget that. One day the Nazis will be defeated and we will proudly remove the sailing ship, display the photograph of our king and sing the national anthem again.' Then she put the sailing ship picture back on the wall and returned to her desk. The class loved this little ceremony. It gave them hope that one day soon they would be free. Now they felt ready to carry on with their lessons.

On this particular morning, Mrs Gray lifted a large box onto her desk.

'Gather round everyone, I have something new for you today,' she said. The children moved round her desk, eagerly waiting to find out what was in the box. 'A ship has come from France with paper and pencils for you.'

What a surprise! All the paper in the school had been used up, so whatever they wrote had to be rubbed out and the paper used again the next day. Everyone got very excited as Mrs Gray gave them each a pencil and a small notebook full of very thin paper with squares on it.

'These pencils are very scratchy, so you mustn't press hard or you will make holes in the paper.' she warned the children. Then she got out an old atlas for them to see.

'Look at this,' she said, opening it up to a page showing a map of Europe. 'Richard, can you find Jersey for me please?' Richard peered at the map and pointed to a tiny dot just below England.

'That's right, well done. And here's Guernsey, Alderney and Sark, the only parts of Great Britain to be occupied by the Germans. And look, here's France, Denmark, Holland, Luxembourg, Belgium, Poland and Norway. All these countries are occupied too and there may be more by now, I just don't know.'

'Mrs Gray, where's Manchester? That's where Simon went,' Jack asked.

'Try to find it yourself, Jack; I'll give you a clue. First find Jersey and then go north.' Jack soon found the city half way up through England. It was a long way away.

'Do you think the German bomber planes we see flying towards England could go as far as Manchester and drop bombs there?' he asked.

'Yes, I think they could. We must hope and pray that all our families in England stay safe,' Mrs Gray replied, shutting the atlas. 'I hope we'll get letters from them soon.' Jack hoped so too; they still had not heard anything from his cousins.

'Well, back to your seats please, it's time for maths,' said Mrs Gray. Jack didn't like maths very much and today he found it very hard to concentrate. He kept thinking of Caroline and wondered what the Germans would do to her; he felt scared now that he knew the bomber planes could bomb Manchester, and he really hoped that they would hear from Uncle Bill saying that the whole family was safe.

At lunch time it was still wet and windy and everyone was very cold. There was a small stove in the corner of the room, but they had run out of wood. Now the fire was out. Mrs Gray pulled her shawl tightly around her and the boys and girls put on their coats, but they couldn't concentrate as they shivered and shook. Soon Mr Richardson decided that it was too cold for the children to stay at school.

'We can't have you shivering all afternoon,' he said. 'If your mums and dads have a few spare logs for our fires, please bring them with you tomorrow.'

So Lizzie met Jack in the playground and they were

nearly blown home by the storm. On the way they picked up twigs that had fallen in the wind, ready to take to school in the morning.

'I didn't expect to see you at this time,' said Mum, as they came into the kitchen. 'My, you are wet! Hurry up and change, then come and warm up by the stove.

'Mr & Mrs Taylor have been deported to Germany just because they're English. I hope they'll be alright,' said Lizzie, as she came back into the kitchen.

"I know, Lizzie, quite a few families have been sent away. I'm so pleased Uncle Bill decided to leave before the war began,' Mum replied. 'This is a dreadful thing that the Germans have done.'

'What will happen to them?' asked Jack.

'I really don't know, it's very worrying indeed,' Mum said, as she gave them a cup of hot milk to drink. For a while nobody spoke as they thought about their friends and family so far away.

'What did you do at school today?' asked Mum, sitting down at the table with her children.

'We had to learn some German,' said Lizzie, pulling a face. 'Miss Benest doesn't want to teach it to us, but the inspector is coming to test us soon.'

'Yes I know, love. All children have to learn it when they reach the age of twelve.'

'But it's the enemy's language,' moaned Lizzie.

'I know. I wish you didn't have to learn it too, but it's just something you have to do. Now tell me something good that's happened today!'

'We've swapped books with another school, so I've got a new story to read,' Lizzie replied.

'And we've got new notebooks and pencils,' said Jack.

'And the German soldiers living next to the playing field told Mr Richardson that we can use it again when they're not playing football,' said Lizzie. Jack hadn't heard this. It was the best news of all!

'There you are. It has been a good day for both of you. And Jack, what do you think of the shoes?' she said, with a twinkle in her eye.

'Fine,' he answered. His feet were dry so he was actually quite pleased to have Maman's shoes after all!

As Lizzie helped Mum lay the table for their supper, she thought about her school friends Ani and Laura.

'You're very quiet, is something worrying you?' asked Mum, who had been watching her daughter.

'Well, it's Ani and Laura. There's something wrong with both of them. Ani fell asleep at her desk today and she keeps forgetting things. She's always so tired and I'm scared that she might be sick.'

'And what about Laura?' asked Mum, feeling very concerned.

'She's very thin and keeps complaining of tummy ache. Her stomach rumbles really loudly in class and the boys keep teasing her.'

'It sounds as if they are both very, very hungry, Lizzie,' answered Mum. 'Ani and her mum don't have a garden to grow vegetables in and with five children in Laura's family, there can't be much food for them all.'

'Laura's worried about her Dad too. He's been arrested for arguing with a soldier and she thinks that he'll be sent to prison, then what will they do?' Lizzie asked, wiping tears from her eyes.

'A lot of families are suffering now. There isn't enough food in the island, and people seem to be getting punished for such little things,' said Mum, shaking her head sadly.

'Can we give them some potatoes and flour, and maybe a rabbit or two?' asked Lizzie.

'Well, we're not meant to do that, but I'm sure we can give them a little bit each week. I'll speak to Dad.'

'Thanks Mum,' said Lizzie, hoping that her Dad would agree.

'Would you like them to stay with us for a few days?'

Mum asked. 'We could really feed them up and I'm sure they would like to help with the animals.'

'Yes, yes!' said Lizzie, flinging her arms around Mum's neck. 'Thank you, Mum.'

When Ani and Laura arrived a few days later, they were very excited as they had never stayed on a farm before. They had porridge for breakfast then played in the fields, enjoying the fresh air. They searched for acorns to be roasted and ground into a powder to make a drink rather like coffee, fed the hens and collected their eggs to eat for supper.

'What can we do now?' asked Laura as she put the eggs in a bowl.

'Well, if you pick enough blackberries, you can help me make a pie,' said Maman.

Lizzie giggled as the two girls rushed outside.

'They've forgotten to take a basket to put the blackberries in,' she said laughingly, as she ran out to find them.

A few hours later, the lovely smell of delicious blackberry and apple pie filled the kitchen and after eating boiled eggs, a slice of bread and a piece of pie, Laura and Ani went to bed feeling full and happy. They fell asleep as soon as their heads touched their pillows and didn't wake up again until the sun was shining through the window and it was time for a lovely bowl of porridge again.

All through the morning, they helped Mum scrub and wash lots and lots of potatoes.

'What are you going to do with them?' asked Ani.

'Well, once they are very clean, we'll take them to Mr Le Brun, who has a huge potato crushing machine,' Mum explained.

'But why do you need to crush them?' asked Laura.

'Once they're crushed, we'll put the pulp onto a big clean sheet on the lawn and let it dry in the sun. Then it will be ready to use as flour for our bread and cakes,' Mum replied. 'We have some ready in the pantry, so would you like to help me make some bread for you to take home to your families?

'Yes please, thank you,' they both replied.

After three days it was time to go home and Laura's tummy hadn't rumbled at all.

'Thank you for letting me stay,' she said, giving Mum a hug.

'I hope you'll both come again,' Mum replied, delighted that the girls looked so well.

'I'd love to come again,' Ani said, with a big beam across her face. Mum gave each of them a pie, a loaf of bread and some eggs to take home. As they said goodbye and walked happily up the drive, Lizzie watched and felt very content.

'Thank you, Mum,' she said.

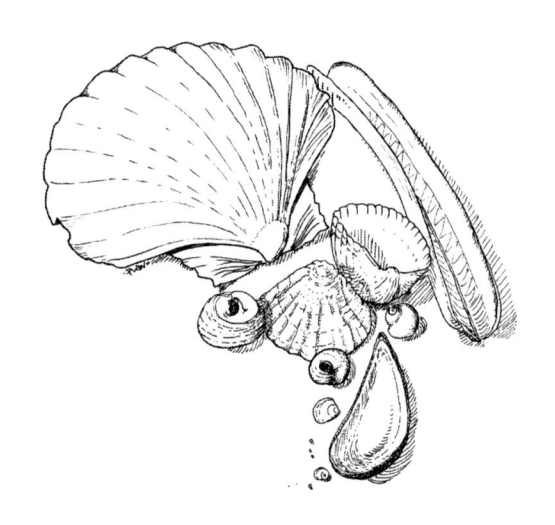

Chapter Nine

Gone Fishing

Poppa was furious, now there was another new rule! The Germans ordered that no one could keep pigeons anymore and Poppa loved his pigeons! Lizzie and Jack had never seen him so angry and looked at their grandmother to see what she would do.

'He's being a very grumpy Poppa!' Maman said. 'He's been grumpy for weeks because the tobacco ration has been cut and now he's cross because he has to get rid of his pigeons. Just keep away from him for a while and let him calm down.' But Poppa would not calm down at all and he refused to kill his pigeons.

'You have to obey them,' said Maman. 'The Germans really seem to think that you could send your pigeons to England carrying messages to the government.'

'Ridiculous! Do they think I'll attach messages to their legs and tell them to fly to London! How would they know where to go?' he roared.

'I know that your pigeons would never fly that far, but the Germans don't know that. Stop being so silly. You're making such a fuss!'

'But I've been breeding my pigeons for years. I know all their names,' Poppa replied angrily, getting really red in the face. He sucked at his thin lips, craving a cigarette. 'Ridiculous!' he said again and stormed out of the house and down the lane.

'Just leave him,' said Maman, 'he'll calm down in time.'

But a few days later the family sat at the table eating pigeon pie, trying not to think of the birds that had lived in the yard for so long.

'Where's Poppa?' asked Jack.

'He's stayed in the cottage, he couldn't bring himself to eat his precious birds,' replied Dad. 'Actually, he was puffing away on a cigarette when I last saw him. Where did he get that from, Maman?'

'Well,' answered Maman, looking very amused. 'He doesn't know it, but I gave Mr Le Brun a pigeon in exchange for that cigarette.' They all laughed, Poppa wouldn't be happy with that if he found out what Maman had done!

Occasionally there was exciting news. The Germans were allowing people to go onto a few of the rocky beaches to collect shellfish to eat. The farmers could also collect seaweed called vraic to use as fertilizer on their fields. Dad was very pleased about this and told Charles to get the horse and cart ready to take to the beach. Even Poppa cheered up and agreed to take Jack and Lizzie too.

'Me too, Poppa!' said Thomas, pulling on his grandfather's trouser leg.

'Sorry, Thomas, not today,' he replied.

'I want to come!' Thomas said, stamping his foot and starting to cry. Poppa picked him up and gave him a big kiss.

'We'll bring a present back for you, it will be a surprise,' he said. Thomas kicked and screamed as Poppa put him down and went out into the hall.

'Poor Thomas, he's three years old and he's never been to the beach,' he said, as he shut the kitchen door. 'Hurry up you two, let's go! Today I'm going to collect winkles and limpets from the rocks, then we'll boil them for our tea!'

'Yuck!' said Lizzie, laughing and pulling a face. 'I'd rather have prawns!'

'And I want to find loads of razorfish!' shouted Jack, as he picked up his bucket and ran across the yard, with Scratch barking and running off ahead of him.

It felt like a holiday as they went up the drive and along the lane, chatting to neighbours and friends all heading for the beach. Even though German soldiers were on guard along the way, everyone was determined to have a few hours of fun.

'Wait for me,' Poppa called, puffing and blowing as he tried to keep up with the two excited children.

'Come on, Poppa,' Lizzie said, running back and taking hold of his hand. 'I'll help you.'

Jack raced ahead with Scratch who went quite mad, barking and digging holes in the sand, sending it in all directions. They ran down to the sea and joined other children from the village, laughing and screaming and splashing each other. Jack threw stones for Scratch and skimmed flat pebbles across the still blue water, watching them bounce before disappearing down to the sand.

Lizzie decided to stay with Poppa, fishing for prawns

in the pools, while he collected limpets and winkles that were clinging to the rocks. He started whistling and didn't even miss his cigarettes.

After a while, Jack got tired of playing in the sea, so he collected some water in his bucket and searched for little holes in the sand that looked like keyholes in a door. He poured some seawater into them and grabbed the long thin razor fish that popped out. As he kicked some seaweed that had been washed up by the tide, he found three cuttlefish shells hidden beneath it.

'Look what I've found, Poppa!' he called, waving them in the air for his grandfather to see.

'Well done lad,' Poppa replied. 'Mum will be very pleased with those cuttlefish! She can heat them in the oven and crush them into powder to make toothpaste for us all.'

'Let's collect some shells and put them in a jam jar to give to Mum for her birthday,' suggested Lizzie, coming down to join him.

'That's a good idea, she'll love that,' Jack replied. So the two children searched for empty shells to give to Mum. They found two big whelks that looked like enormous snails, cockle shells, limpets and, best of all, beautiful winkles of all different colours – yellow, orange, white, pink, striped and brown – they knew that Mum would be very pleased with her present.

Poppa picked up a piece of driftwood, sat on Jack's favourite rock and got his penknife out of his pocket. As he carved the wood he watched his grandchildren. It was so good to see them laughing and playing on the beach again.

After a while, he asked them to come and sit with him. They showed him their shells and then snuggled up against his shoulders. As they watched, the wood he was carving began to look like a little boat.

'Is that for Thomas?' Lizzie asked.

'Yes, I promised that I'd bring him a present. Do you think he'll like it?'

'Yes, Poppa, I'm sure he will,' Lizzie replied.

They sat enjoying the sunshine, watching the waves and looking out across the water to France. A warship, painted in camouflage colours, light grey, dark grey and white, was anchored in the bay and in the distance, they could see a cargo boat, hopefully bringing food and clothes to the island.

'I wonder what Simon's doing now?' said Jack, as he thought about all the happy times they had had together sitting on this rock. 'When will they come home, Poppa?'

Poppa sighed. 'I don't know, Jack. I hope they'll be

back soon. This war has gone on far too long,' he said, putting his arms around them. 'I'm an old man now and I want to see Jersey free again before I die.'

'Of course you will, Poppa. It won't be long now, I'm sure it won't,' answered Lizzie, looking up into his sad eyes.

'I hope you're right love. I hope you're right.'

'Then we will be able to take the sailing ship picture down,' said Jack.

'What do you mean?' asked Poppa.

'Well, we've got a big picture of a ship in the classroom and there's a secret...' Jack stopped and looked away as he realised he shouldn't have said anything at all.

Lizzie was very curious. 'What secret?' she asked.

'I'm not meant to say anything,' answered Jack, kicking the sand with his foot. Lizzie got up and stood in front of her brother.

'Come on, tell us, Jack,' she said, poking him hard on his arm.

'Ouch! Go away. I can't tell you, I promised. We all did,' Jack replied, pushing her so hard that she fell onto the sand.

'Poppa, make him tell us,' cried Lizzie.

'That's enough both of you,' said Poppa, 'if you've been told not to say anything, Jack, that's fine. Come on, it's time to go home, we'll have a feast tonight!'

'But Poppa!' Lizzie exclaimed as she brushed the sand off her clothes. 'That's not fair!'

'That's enough, Lizzie,' said Poppa sternly. And with that, he walked up the beach with Jack, leaving a very cross Lizzie slowly following on behind.

As they walked up the lane, Jack felt sad that he couldn't tell his family about the king hidden behind the picture, but he knew that one day, when the Germans left the island, he would be able to show them what it was all about.

When they got home, Lizzie disappeared upstairs to sulk and Jack showed Mum all they had collected (apart from the beautiful shells hidden in his pocket). She was very pleased with the shellfish and was soon preparing their supper.

Thomas was happy to see them too. He ran to Poppa and put out his hands. 'Where's my present, Poppa?' he asked.

Poppa lifted him onto his knee and gave him the boat. 'What do you think this is, Thomas?' he asked lovingly. Thomas studied it carefully, turning it round and round in his hands.

'It's a boat!'

'Yes, and we'll sail it on the stream tomorrow,'

answered Poppa with a smile.

'I like this boat,' said Thomas, as he flung his arms around his grandfather's neck.

'That's good,' laughed Poppa; 'very good indeed!'

After a while, Dad came into the kitchen with more good news.

'Look, Poppa! This should cheer you up!' he said, opening a small yellow tin. 'Tobacco – see! It's been brought here from France.'

Poppa was delighted. 'Thanks son,' he said, taking the tin and putting it safely in his pocket. He sighed contentedly and went to the stove where the fish was cooking.

'Well, the prawns and shellfish are ready and I have tobacco in my pocket. It really has been a wonderful day!'

Chapter Ten

Jack is Sick

Jack woke up feeling hot and sticky. He had a sore throat, his head hurt and he felt very unwell. Scratch nudged him, but he didn't get out of bed. Scratch couldn't understand this at all. Normally, Jack jumped up and played with him before they ran downstairs together, but today he just turned over and buried his head in his pillow. A few minutes later Mum opened the door.

'Jack, I've called you three times, hurry up!' But Jack did not move. 'Jack, what's wrong, love?' she asked, sitting on the edge of his bed. He turned over and looked at his mother. Her face looked blurred and her voice sounded strange. He felt very peculiar. Mum put her hand on his forehead.

'Oh dear, you have a high temperature. No school for you today. I'll get you a drink of water which should make you feel a bit better.' She went downstairs looking very worried and found Dad eating his breakfast in the kitchen.

'Jack's really poorly,' she said. 'I've heard that three other children in his class at school are also ill. I wonder what's the matter with them all.'

'If he's not better in a day or two, we can call Dr Brown,' Dad replied, hoping that Jack would be up and about by dinner time.

But Jack did not feel better by dinner time or even by the next day – in fact, he felt worse. His head still hurt, his throat was so sore that it was painful to swallow and his voice sounded croaky. He kept feeling hot then very cold and had a horrible cough that sounded rather like Scratch's bark. At times, he found it hard to breath and that was very scary.

Mum called Dr Brown, who drove down the drive in his little black car. He was a kind man who smiled a lot. Jack liked him.

'Hello Jack,' he said. 'I hear that you are not feeling too well.' He touched Jack's forehead. 'Oh dear, you are very hot. Is your throat sore?' Jack nodded. It hurt too much to talk.

'Mmm,' said the doctor. 'Well, my lad, you've caught a nasty bug called diphtheria. I'll give you some medicine that will help you to feel better very soon.' He patted Jack on the head and went downstairs with Mum.

'He really is extremely sick, Jane,' he said, looking very serious. 'Here's his medicine and try to get him to have a drink. That should help.'

'Thank you, Doctor,' said Mum, taking the big bottle of medicine from him.

'Diphtheria is very infectious,' said Dr Brown, climbing into his car. 'I've been to see five other children who have all caught it. It's important that Lizzie and Thomas don't go in to see him.'

'I'll make sure they keep away,' Mum replied. 'Goodbye.'

'I'll come back to see him tomorrow,' called Dr Brown as he drove away.

For five days only Scratch was allowed to keep him company when Mum was busy downstairs. He sat patiently by Jack's bed, waiting for him to play. Jack was pleased that Scratch stayed, but he didn't even want to stroke him. He just lay there. He could hear the farmyard sounds in the distance – ducks quacking and the cockerel crowing; Lizzie and Maman laughing and Dad, Poppa and Charles chatting as they brought the cows in for milking. Everything seemed a long way away and he wasn't interested in any of it. All he wanted to do was sleep, but the cough, cough, coughing went on and on, keeping him awake and very unhappy.

Dad decided to kill one of their precious chickens so that Mum could make chicken broth, hoping that this would make Jack feel a bit better. He sat on his son's bed with a bowl of hot broth in his hand.

'Come on, son, please try to drink this. It will help you get strong again.' So with Dad's help Jack sat up, but cough, cough, cough he went again.

'Just one spoonful, please try,' said Dad encouragingly. Jack sipped the broth. Yes, it was good, even though it hurt his throat to swallow. He tried again and had a bit more. The warm broth felt good in his tummy and he lay down and fell asleep.

Each day, Mum sat by his bed and read the adventures of William Brown and his scruffy dog Jumble. The Just William stories were his favourite and as she read, he felt comfy and special having his mum to himself for a change.

'Well, he actually sat up and listened to the story today,' Mum told the family as they sat round the table at dinner time. 'You know, I think he is a little better.'

Soon Jack began to feel rather bored, which his mother said was a very good sign. He felt well enough to get up and look out of the window. Scratch jumped up and wagged his tail as Jack stroked him.

'Thank you for staying with me, Scratch,' he said, as he scratched the happy dog behind his ears. 'I'm sorry that I couldn't talk to you, my throat hurt so much.' Scratch licked Jack's face with delight; he was just pleased to have his friend to play with again.

'Mum will let me go outside soon, and then we'll go to the woods. Does that sound like a good idea?' Jack asked. Scratch put a paw on his knee and gave a little bark which made Jack laugh. 'I think that meant yes. I'm glad you agree!'

Just then, Jack heard a noise coming from the yard. He looked out of the window and saw his friend Richard sitting on his bike, ringing its bell and looking up at the window, trying to get his attention.

'Jack! Can you come out to play?' called Richard. Jack shook his head. 'I've brought my old comics for you to read, shall I give them to your mum?' he asked, holding up a copy of Dandy for him to see. Jack nodded and grinned at his friend. He was very excited to have something new to read.

Later that day, as he sat by the window enjoying the adventures of Desperate Dan the cowboy, who was the strongest man in the world and could lift up a cow with one hand, Dr Brown came into the room.

'Well, Jack, you certainly look much better today,' said Dr Brown.

'Yes, Dr Brown, I feel fine now. Please can I go downstairs?'

'Keep drinking the broth and in two days' time you can go downstairs, Jack,' Dr Brown replied with a smile.

'Thank you,' said Jack – he just couldn't wait!

Two days seemed a very long time now that he felt well again. He stood on the window sill and watched the hustle and bustle that was going on in the yard and the fields beyond. It was harvest time and Mum, Dad, Poppa, Charles and Lizzie, were all busy in the fields. Three other farmers were helping too, as they cut the wheat and the barley. Then, they put it in a threshing machine and collected the grain to be made into flour, tied the stalks into bundles and piled them up to make haystacks in the fields. He really wished that he could join everyone outside.

But the following morning everything changed. Thomas began to cough – just like he had two weeks before. Everyone was very worried and Dad kept coming back from the fields to find out how his little boy was. Jack crept into Lizzie's bedroom and they could hear Thomas's cough and strange little cry as he struggled to breathe. They realised that he was very, very sick. They tiptoed onto the landing and crouched down to look through the banisters. Mum was holding Thomas in her arms, rocking him like a little baby.

'There, there,' she whispered in his ear 'Shhh, go to sleep, Thomas, Mummy's here.' But Thomas was hot and restless and just kept on coughing.

'You'd better call Dr Brown, John. Tell him to come quickly, Thomas is really bad.'

They watched as Dad grabbed his coat, ran out into the yard, jumped onto his bike and peddled as fast as he could up the drive. Dr Brown soon arrived; he took one look at Thomas and shook his head.

'You were right to call me, Thomas has caught diphtheria and he's very poorly.' He gently put his hand on Mum's shoulder. 'I'm so sorry, Jane, but I don't have any medicine to give him,' he said sadly.

'Surely you can get some of the medicine you gave to

Jack. The hospital must have it,' said Mum anxiously.

'I rang the hospital this morning; there isn't any left on the island. I'm so sorry.'

'But he's only three years old, we have to help him. What can we do?' asked Mum, hugging Thomas tight and trying not to cry.

'Give him sips of water and keep him as cool as you can. Maybe he'll be able to fight this on his own,' answered Dr Brown. 'I'll come back in the morning.' He said goodbye and soon Jack heard his car drive off into the distance.

That evening, Mum did not leave the kitchen at all. She paced up and down with Thomas in her arms coughing, her quiet voice trying to comfort him.

'I wish we had some of your medicine left to give him,' whispered Lizzie. Jack had not thought of this and suddenly felt very upset.

'He's only tiny; he needs it more than I did,' he replied.

'You needed it too, Jack,' said Lizzie. 'Sometimes you coughed so loudly that I had to put my pillow over my head so that I could get to sleep!'

'Really?' said Jack in surprise. Lizzie nodded and they turned their thoughts back to Thomas.

'He'll be alright,' she said quietly. 'Come on, let's go

to bed.'

Very early the next morning, as the sun appeared over the horizon, the cockerel crowed loudly in the farmyard and Jack woke up with a start. He listened. Apart from the noisy bird, everything was quiet. 'Everyone must be asleep,' he thought. 'That's good, Thomas must be feeling better.' He flung back the covers, grabbed his dressing gown and went across the corridor to Lizzie's room.

'Lizzie, wake up! Thomas has stopped coughing, he must be asleep,' he said excitedly. Lizzie stretched and rubbed her eyes.

'Let's go and see,' she suggested. The two children crept to Thomas's room, carefully avoiding the creaky floor board and opened the door, but Thomas was not there.

Lizzie frowned. 'That's strange,' she exclaimed, staring at the empty bed. Jack peeped through the keyhole of Mum and Dad's door, but no one was there either.

'They must be downstairs. Come on,' he said.

'Shhh, listen!' whispered Lizzie as they reached the closed kitchen door. Someone was crying, but it wasn't Thomas's cry. They quietly opened the door then stopped, frightened and confused by what they saw.

Dad was standing by the stove with his arms wrapped around Mum who was sobbing. He stroked her hair and Jack could see that tears were running down his face too. Charles was standing by the window looking very uncomfortable; Maman was sitting at the kitchen table with her head in her hands and Poppa looked very serious as he patted her hand. Lizzie and Jack looked around the room - Thomas was not there. Suddenly, they knew that something terrible had happened and they grabbed hold of each other, unsure of what they should do next.

'Mum, Dad,' said Lizzie with a little shaky voice. 'What's happened?' But no one replied. Lizzie ran to her mum and burst into tears. 'Mum,' she shouted, shaking her arm. 'Where's Thomas? Tell me what's happened.' Mum turned, her eyes were red and her face all blotchy.

'Oh Lizzie my love, he's gone, he's gone,' she cried, putting her arms round her daughter.

Jack looked from one face to the other; he didn't understand. 'Gone where?' he asked no one in particular.

'Come here, Jack,' said Dad, wiping away his tears. 'You know that Thomas was very sick yesterday. Well, his little body was not strong enough to fight the germs.

Thomas has gone to heaven.'

'What do you mean, gone to heaven?' Jack cried. 'I want to see Thomas.'

'No Jack, I'm sorry you can't. Thomas died in the night.' Jack couldn't speak. How could this happen to his little brother? Then, he had a terrible thought. He gasped, pulled away from his father's arms and ran out of the kitchen and up the stairs and into his room. He flung himself onto his bed, buried his face in the pillow and sobbed. Had Thomas caught the cough from him?

'I'm sorry, Thomas,' he cried. 'I didn't mean to hurt you; I didn't mean to hurt you!' Dad had followed him up the stairs and sat on his bed.

'Jack, it's not your fault. Never think that.'

'But I got sick first, so Thomas caught it from me,' he cried.

'No, Jack. Look at me,' said Dad, pulling Jack up and holding him tight. 'We don't know how he caught this illness. It could have been at the shop or in church last Sunday. He might even have caught it at the same time as you; it just took longer to make him ill.' Dad wiped the tears from Jack's eyes. 'I know you would never, ever hurt him. We all know that. Please believe me son.'

'He could have had my medicine,' Jack said through his sobs.

'You needed it too, Jack,' Dad said. 'You mustn't blame yourself.'

'But I want him back,' sobbed Jack.

'I know, I know. We all do. We will always miss him very much,' Dad replied. 'Come downstairs with me, we all need to be together on a sad day like this.' Dad took hold of his son's hand and together they went back into the kitchen.

Jack stared at the rug by the stove. That was where Thomas always played. Now it just looked old, torn and ugly. And his little brother would never play on it again.

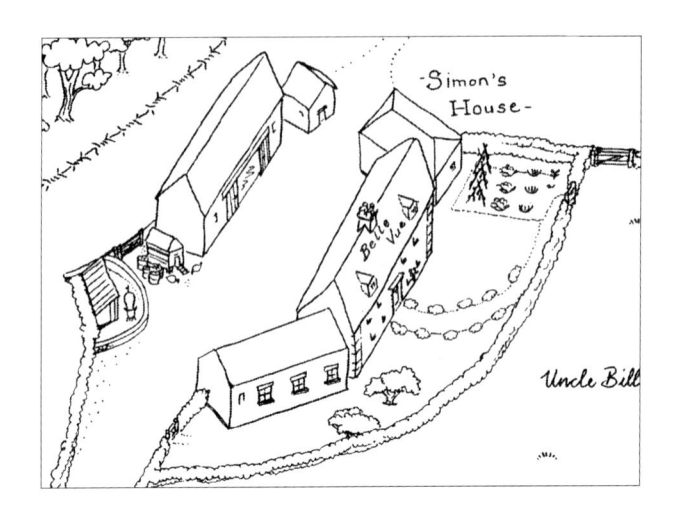

Chapter Eleven

Scratch Goes Missing

Christmas was a very sad time for the family as they all missed Thomas very much indeed. It took Jack a long time to accept that he had not made Thomas sick and he really missed his little brother.

'We'll never forget Thomas,' Dad said, as he watched his son push Thomas's toy tractor across the floor. 'We must remember all the fun times we had with him.'

'I know, Dad, but I still feel so sad sometimes,' Jack

replied.

'Me too,' answered Dad. 'I like to remember his funny little ways, like lining up the vegetables on his plate and counting them before he would eat them.'

'But he could only count to four, so then he started at one again!' interrupted Jack.

'And using Maman's walking stick as a horse!' Dad said with a laugh.

'He called the stick Bobby, didn't he, Dad?' said Jack, as he pictured his brother galloping round the yard.

Dad looked down at him. 'You're right, he did. Try to remember these happy times, Jack. You know he'll always be your brother, even though he's not here now.' Jack thought for a moment. Yes, he had lots of very happy memories.

'I'll try,' he replied.

One cold, icy morning a few months later, Jack woke up and called Scratch, who usually bounded into the bedroom and jumped onto his bed wagging his tail, but this time he didn't come. Jack ran downstairs and into the kitchen.

'Slow down, what's the rush?' asked Mum.

'It's Scratch, he didn't come up to my room this morning. Have you seen him?' he asked.

'No, I thought he was with you,' Mum replied. 'Maybe he went out with Dad and Poppa. They've just finished the milking.'

Jack raced outside, slipping and sliding on the frozen puddles and searched the yard. Scratch was nowhere to be seen. He found Dad in the field as he hammered a large peg into the ground then tethered Bluebell, the oldest cow in the herd, onto it with a long, thick rope.

'Dad,' he called, 'I can't find Scratch, have you seen him?'

'No, come to think of it, I haven't seen him this morning,' Dad replied.

'Have you looked in the meadow?' asked Poppa, as he threw a large sack blanket over one of the cows to keep it warm and snug. 'I'll be very cross with him if he's chasing the chickens.'

'Scratch, you silly dog, where are you?' Jack called again. But Scratch was not in the meadow either. He was really worried now. 'I hope nothing bad has happened to him.' he said to himself.

Just then, Charles ran out of the house to join him. 'Wait for me, Jack,' he called. 'Let's look in the woods.'

Jack was pleased to have his cousin's company and together they crossed the frozen stream, calling as they went. When they reached the old oak tree they climbed up into the branches for a better look.

'Look!' said Charles, pointing towards Belle Vue. 'There's smoke coming from one of the chimneys. There must be someone living there.'

'Are you sure?' said Jack in surprise. 'There wasn't anyone there when we fed the pigs yesterday.' But sure enough, smoke was swirling upwards into the blue sky.

'The Germans must have moved in, we'd better tell Dad,' said Jack, jumping down and turning to go back home.

'No, come on, let's find out what's happening. Maybe Scratch saw the smoke too and thought Simon had come home,' Charles said. So they set off towards the farm, creeping through the grass until they reached an old iron gate that led into the farm yard. Someone had closed the gate and Charles slowly lifted the heavy latch, which creaked and groaned. They stopped and held their breath, hoping that no one had heard. But no one came. Carefully pushing open the gate, they tiptoed into the corner of the yard and hid behind a pile of potato barrels. From there, they could see four cars, a lorry and lots of German soldiers busily going in and out of the house.

'This way,' whispered Charles, leading Jack through a small doorway into the barn. 'If we climb up that ladder and look through the tiny window at the far end of the loft, we might be able to see what they're doing. I'll go first, then you follow me.' Jack could feel his heart thumping as he climbed up the rickety ladder into the hayloft. He peered out of the window and to his surprise, on the back door step of Simon's house, sat a soldier talking to Scratch, who was wagging his tail with happiness. The man threw a ball and Scratch ran after it and took it back to him, dropping it at his feet and waiting for more. The soldier patted him and gave him something to eat. He seemed to like the dog and was talking kindly to him.

'We've got to get him back,' said Jack, feeling really worried. 'Scratch shouldn't be with the enemy, it isn't right!'

'Scratch doesn't know he's the enemy, silly. He just likes to play,' Charles replied. But Jack was not at all happy. The enemy had taken over Belle Vue and now they had his dog!

Suddenly Jack felt a tickle in his nose and he sneezed an enormous sneeze. Charles pulled him down into the hay, but that made him sneeze again and again. Suddenly, they heard Scratch bark.

'He must have heard you sneeze, now we're in big trouble,' said Charles angrily, hitting Jack hard on his back.

'I'm sorry, I'm really sorry,' sniffed Jack, who was terrified now. The barking got louder and louder and soon they heard Scratch at the bottom of the ladder. They both froze with fear.

'Who is there?' someone called. 'Come down now!'

Charles and Jack knew there was no way to escape. They slowly crossed the loft and looked down at a very excited Scratch and a very serious soldier.

'What are you doing?' asked the soldier, pointing his long brown rifle at them. 'Come down!' he ordered again. They carefully climbed down the old ladder and stood in front of the soldier. Jack's hands were sweaty and his legs were trembling. He had heard of children being taken to the Nazi headquarters and parents having to go there to collect them. Sometimes the parents were put into jail for what their children had done.

'You must not be here,' said the soldier sternly.

'We - we were looking for our dog,' answered Charles, trying to be very brave in front of his young cousin.

'He is yours?' asked the soldier, pointing at Scratch. 'I see that he likes you!' The soldier lowered the gun.

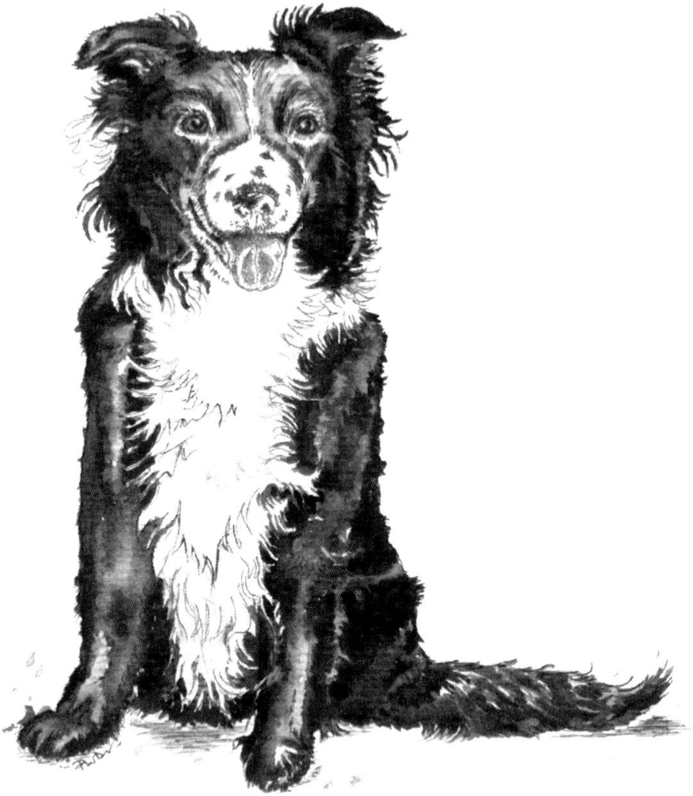

'His name?' Jack tried to answer but he was so scared that only a tiny croak came out of his mouth.

'He's called Scratch,' answered Charles.

'Scratch,' repeated the soldier, kneeling down and patting him. 'Nice dog.' Jack had a weird feeling that he couldn't quite understand. In a strange sort of way he liked this soldier because the soldier liked Scratch. But in another way he still felt really cross that Scratch had being playing with one of the Germans. He wondered whether this man could possibly be just an ordinary man like his dad. It was all very confusing.

'You go now, not come back,' said the soldier. 'Goodbye, Scratch.' With that, he pointed his gun at them to show that he really meant what he said, then turned and walked back to the house.

'Thank you, sir,' said Charles politely. 'Come on, Scratch.' The two boys turned and ran out of the yard as fast as they could, with Scratch bounding along beside them. They didn't stop until they reached the old oak tree, where they sat leaning against the tree trunk, out of breath and feeling very shaky.

'That was a lucky escape,' said Jack.

'Yes, but because you sneezed, we still don't know what they're doing at the farm,' Charles replied.

'It's not my fault that I sneezed,' answered Jack

indignantly. 'Do you think soldiers live there now?'

'Probably,' answered Charles. 'But there were too many of them for it to be an ordinary home, and I think those were officers' cars in the yard. Something is going on and we need to find out what it is.'

'We've got to tell Dad,' said Jack.

'No, I don't think that's a good idea,' answered Charles. 'Let's not tell the grown-ups until we've found out more.'

When they got home, Dad was just leaving in the van, pulled by Robin and Chestnut.

'Where's he going?' asked Jack.

'The Germans have told him to collect Uncle Bill's pigs, so he's bringing them back here,' answered Lizzie.

'Why?' asked Jack, pretending to be surprised.

'I think they've moved into the farm house,' she replied.

'Oh have they?' said Charles. 'I wonder what they're doing.' He glanced at Jack, signalling for him to stay quiet. He was determined to discover the truth.

Chapter Twelve

The Man In The Woods

Belle Vue was now surrounded by a barbed wire fence. Dad told the children that they were not to go anywhere near it, but Jack and Charles still wanted to know what was going on. Sometimes they disobeyed and crept along the fence, but there was no way through. There were still lots of soldiers at the farm but it was impossible to see what they were doing.

One morning, Jack had a brilliant idea. 'If I use Dad's binoculars, maybe I'll be able to see the farm from the skylight in the attic,' he thought. He found the binoculars and went up the wooden stairs into the dusty attic. It was full of boxes and bags, old pictures and bits of furniture the family did not use and it smelt a bit too, as every night, Maman struggled up the stairs with her precious turkeys and locked them in the attic so that they wouldn't get stolen.

The tiny window was high up in the roof, so he pushed a large metal box underneath it, then put a little wooden chair on top of the box, but he still couldn't see out. He found some books which he placed on the chair and carefully climbed on top of the wobbly pile. Then he opened the window and stuck his head out, resting his arms on the sill.

Through his binoculars he could see his garden, the stream, his oak tree in the woods and in the distance, up on the hill, the yard at Belle Vue. There were soldiers in the yard and he watched as they roughly pushed some men onto the back of a lorry. Then, one soldier hit a man with his gun and kicked him as he fell onto the ground. Then the soldier climbed into the lorry which disappeared behind the trees, leaving the injured man lying in the yard.

Jack gasped. 'There's no one to help him, he might be dead,' he thought. 'And that lorry went towards the headland. I wonder what they're doing.'

All day long Jack felt very upset by what he had seen. So that night, he waited until Mum and Dad had gone to bed, then crept across the landing to Charles' room to tell him all about it. Charles was fast asleep.

'Charles,' he whispered, shaking his arm. 'Wake up!'

'Go away!' Charles muttered.

'Come on, wake up,' said Jack, a little louder. 'It's important.' Charles yawned.

'What do you want?'

Jack told him about the soldiers, the strange men pushed onto the lorry which drove off towards the headland, and the injured man in the yard. Charles sat up; now he was very interested.

'I'll try to sneak out early tomorrow morning and get a closer look, then I'll come back and tell you what I've found out,' he said.

'I'm coming with you,' said Jack.

'No! You're too young, it could be dangerous,' Charles replied.

'But I saw them first!'

'I said no. Go back to bed, Jack.'

Jack was very, very cross. He sat on his bed and sulked. How dare Charles say he was too young! He was not a baby; in fact, he was eleven years old and felt very grown up. He decided that he would have to follow Charles, so he put on his outdoor clothes and sat on the floor by the door.

He waited and waited, struggling to stay awake. Then, just as the sun came up over the horizon, he heard Charles creep downstairs, open the door into the yard and close it again. Jack tiptoed down to the kitchen and Scratch bounded up to him wanting to play.

'Shhh, quiet Scratch. Stay!' he whispered, as he went out into the yard. He knew that the curfew wouldn't be over for two more hours and he shouldn't be outside, but as quietly as he could, he followed his cousin. They went through the dark woods until they reached the bushes that grew on the steep bank leading to the barbed wire fence. Then Charles stopped and Jack slowly moved towards him. Suddenly, he knelt on a twig which snapped noisily beneath his knee. Charles looked round and Jack could see the terrified look on his face.

'It's only me,' he said in a loud whisper.

'I told you not to come,' said Charles, angrily. Jack just grinned.

'Well I'm here now, so you'll have to put up with it!'

'Just be quiet and do as I say,' ordered Charles.

The two boys fought their way through the bushes and when they reached the fence, Charles lay down and carefully tugged it apart, making a hole just big enough for them to wriggle through. They slowly pulled themselves forward on their elbows, then parted the bracken. Now they could see what the Germans had been doing. There, built on the rocks just below the top of the headland was a massive, tall, round concrete bunker just like many others around the coast It had huge thick grey walls with slits in them like windows without glass and they could just see the top of a big metal door. A man was standing on top of the tower looking out to sea through his binoculars.

'Wow, it's huge!' exclaimed Jack.

'It's one of their observation towers. They've got a good view of France from there,' whispered Charles. 'They must be looking out for British ships that might try to rescue us.'

The boys watched as three officers got out of a car that was parked on the headland. The two soldiers guarding the tower stood to attention and raised their right arms in salute. Then the officers went down some steps and disappeared inside. Jack looked around, he was puzzled; the men he had seen from the attic were not there.

'I wonder what happened to the people I saw,' he said.

'I think they were prisoners. The Germans bring them from Russia and Poland to build all the bunkers and towers. They're probably back at their camp now,' Charles explained. 'Come on, we've solved the mystery, we'd better get back home before we're missed.'

As they walked back through the woods, Charles tripped over what he thought was a branch and fell full length onto the ground. He heard a groan, then another. There was someone there. Jack just stood and stared, his eyes nearly popping out of his head. On the ground was a very, very thin man. So thin that he looked like a skeleton with skin on. He wore filthy torn clothes, had rags wrapped around his feet and he trembled as he looked from Charles to Jack with frightened eyes.

'Are – are you alright?' asked Charles, getting up and brushing the leaves off his clothes. He knew that was a silly thing to ask. The man was definitely not alright, but he didn't know what else to say.

The man tried to sit up and they helped him lean against a tree. He made chewing movements and pointed to his mouth.

'He's hungry,' said Jack, 'we've got to help him.'

'He must be one of the prisoners. We'll get into

trouble if we're found helping him. Come on, let's go home'

'No! We can't leave him here, he'll starve, Charles. We have to help!'

'It's too dangerous.'

'You go home if you want to, but I'm staying here!' said Jack, staring at his cousin with a determined look that Charles had never seen before.

'Ok, what do you want to do then?' Charles asked.

'We'll carry him to the farm and hide him in the barn. Then we can get him some food. Come on.'

They each took hold of an arm and pulled the man to his feet. He was so weak that he couldn't help himself at all and as he was too tall for Jack to carry, they had to drag him through the woods towards the farm. All of a sudden, they heard German cars in the field heading towards the observation tower.

'Quick! We'll have to hide,' whispered Charles. So they dragged the man back among the trees as he groaned with pain. Once they were well hidden, they sat and waited, hoping the soldiers would go on their way.

'I'll go and see what's happening,' Charles said.

A few minutes later he reported back. 'They're still there. One car has stopped and the soldiers are just smoking cigarettes and laughing together. They don't look as if they'll move for a while.'

'What can we do?' asked Jack, feeling very afraid.

'I climbed up the old oak tree and saw more cars driving towards Les Chenês. They'll see us if we go into the meadow, so we'll have to go through Mr Le Brun's field and past Mr Amy's cottage instead,' Charles explained.

So off they went again. It was much further this way and Jack was exhausted. He just couldn't pull the man any more.

'I can't go any further,' he said, letting go and sitting on the ground.

'You have to! Come on,' Charles replied. 'It was your idea to take him to the farm in the first place, so you can't give up now!'

'He's too heavy and it will take ages to get back to the farm this way.'

'Let's put him in Mr Amy's shed then,' suggested Charles.

Jack took a deep breath and put the man's arm around his shoulders. 'I'll try, let's go!'

'I can do it! I can do it!' he kept saying to himself until they finally reached the shed. Charles opened the door and Jack and the man collapsed in a heap on the floor, knocking over a bucket and some garden tools and making a terrible noise.

Mr Amy, who was sitting in his kitchen, heard the noise and wondered what it was. He looked out of the window just as the shed door closed.

'There's someone in my shed!' he exclaimed and ran outside.

'Who's there?' he called. But no one answered. 'I know you're there, come out this minute!' Charles slowly opened the door again.

'It's me, Charles,' he said, showing himself.

'And what are you doing in my shed?' asked Mr Amy.

'Well – um.'

'Come on, out with it! What are you doing out during curfew?'

'We're just hiding in here, Mr Amy,' answered Charles.

'Why do you need to hide and who have you got in there with you?'

'It's Jack and a man we found in the woods. We want to give him something to eat,' Charles replied.

'Let me see,' said Mr Amy, pushing Charles aside. There was Jack sitting beside the thinnest man he had ever seen. He had long greasy hair, a straggly beard and sore patches on his skin. He was very dirty and smelt absolutely horrid too.

'He's one of the German prisoners,' said Mr Amy, shaking his head. 'Look at him - he's starving. How can anyone treat another human being so badly? Where did you find him?' he asked.

'He was lying in the woods,' answered Jack.

'And what were you doing there during curfew, may I ask?' Charles told Mr Amy the whole story.

'We were taking him back to Les Chênes but there were soldiers in the field, so we hid in your shed,' he explained.

'We've got a big problem. We'll be in serious trouble if we're caught helping a prisoner. Do you realise that since you are both still children, your Dads would be punished too, possibly even deported to a prison camp in Germany or worse still, shot?' The boys hadn't thought of that and began to realise that, by helping the man, they had put their whole families in danger.

Mr Amy put his hand on the man's bony shoulder; he felt so sorry for him and really wanted to help too.

'We won't hurt you,' he said, 'we'll find somewhere for you to rest and give you something to eat.' The man seemed to realise that these were friends and he smiled for the first time.

'It's not safe to stay here as it's too close to the road, but there's a tiny tumbledown shed in the middle of the woods that will make a very good hiding place. It's surrounded by bushes and covered with ivy, nobody will find him there,' said Mr Amy. 'Wait here for a moment.'

He crept back into the house, careful not to wake his wife, who was still sound asleep upstairs, and put some bread, milk, an apple and a bottle of water into a bag. Then, he headed back to the shed and helped Charles carry the man into the woods.

It was getting light and as Jack followed on behind, he could hear the sound of the birds singing loudly in the trees. For just a few moments, he looked at the beautiful spring flowers that were growing everywhere and forgot the soldiers and the man they had found. 'My wood is a beautiful place,' he thought. Then, just as Mr Amy had said, hidden under ivy and with tree branches growing through the broken walls, stood a little granite shed.

'I often come this way but I've never seen it before,' said Jack in surprise.

'Good, so it's the perfect hiding place isn't it?' Mr Amy replied, as they lay the man down on the soft mossy floor and sat with him as he drank and ate for the first time in days.

'Spasiba,' said the man. They didn't understand him, but from the smile on his face they could easily guess that 'thank you' was what he was saying.

Back at Les Chênes, Scratch was lying by the kitchen door waiting for Jack to return. Suddenly, he pricked up his ears and listened. He could hear the sound of a bell clanging in the distance. Once, twice, three times. Then it stopped. Once, twice, three times went the bell again. He barked and scratched at the door, wanting to get out to investigate.

'Be quiet, Scratch!' shouted Dad, who had been woken up by all the noise. Then he heard the ringing too; it was coming from Mr and Mrs Amy's cottage. He had told them to ring the old bell that hung from their roof if there was a real emergency. Something must have happened and they needed him now!

'Jane, fetch Charles! We have to go to Mr Amy's,' shouted Dad, as he ran down the stairs.

'He's not here,' she called over the banisters.

'What do you mean - not here?

'He isn't in his room, and Jack's gone too!'

'Maybe they heard the bell and went to the cottage. They're probably there already. Wait till I see them, they shouldn't have gone out during curfew.'

140

'Be careful, John,' Mum said, as he disappeared into the yard. Dad was worried; worried about Charles and Jack and also wondering why Mr and Mrs Amy needed his help so badly. Maybe one of them had fallen or was sick. Maybe someone had attacked them or there was a fire. Whatever it was, Dad knew that he had to get there as soon as possible.

When he reached the cottage, he banged on the door. The bell stopped ringing and the door opened just enough for him to see Mrs Amy's frightened face.

'Come in quickly,' she sobbed, pulling him inside. 'Oh dear, what a to-do!'

'Please sit down, Mrs Amy,' said Dad, leading her to an old green armchair and puffing up the cushions to make it comfy. 'There, that's better. Start at the beginning and tell me all about it. Where's Mr Amy?"

'That's just it, I don't know! When I woke up, Fred was gone. That was an hour ago and he hasn't come back. Dear oh dear!' She put her hands over her face and cried.

'Have Jack and Charles gone to look for him?'

'I don't know, I haven't' seen them,' she said, blowing her nose on her small blue hankie. 'Maybe he's fallen or the Germans caught him outside before the end of curfew. I'm always telling him not to go out, but he doesn't listen. What a to-do!'

'Please calm down, I'll find him,' said Dad, patting her hand. He made her some acorn coffee and told her not to worry as there was probably a simple explanation.

'I'll be back soon,' he said, but he thought it was all very strange. Mr Amy was missing and so were Charles and Jack. They might be together, but why? He looked in the meadow and went to Jack's favourite tree in the wood, but they were not there. 'Maybe they've gone back to the farm,' he thought and went back home.

Mum was very upset when she heard what had happened and she hurried down to Mrs Amy's cottage to keep her company. Dad had to milk the cows, so decided to search again once that was done.

Back in the woods, the man was looking a little bit better. He had eaten the bread, drunk the milk, and kept repeating, 'Spasiba, Spasiba.' After a while he waved them away with his hand and Mr Amy realised that he wanted them to leave.

'He's telling us to go. I'm sure he knows that we shouldn't be helping him and he doesn't want us to get caught.' So they left him in the hiding place and covered the entrance so that it couldn't be seen.

'I'll bring some more food tomorrow,' said Jack, as

they walked back to the cottage.

'Fred! Thank goodness your back. Where have you been?' asked Mrs Amy, as they walked through the door. 'I've been so worried.'

'It's a long story, but we're fine,' Mr Amy replied. He sat down and told her what had happened, as Charles and Jack looked at Mum and wondered what Dad would have to say.

'You two must come back with me. Dad will want to know all about it,' said Mum.

As they entered in the yard, Scratch began to bark and Dad rushed out of the stable. 'Well! What have you got to say for yourselves?' he asked, crossly. 'Come inside and tell me everything.'

Charles and Jack knew that they had to tell the whole truth, right from the beginning. Dad listened in silence, and then he shook his head.

'I'm sorry, Dad,' said Jack, looking at the floor, waiting to find out what punishment they would receive.

'What were you thinking Charles? By helping a prisoner, the whole family could be deported.'

'Sorry, Uncle John,' said Charles. 'I didn't think...'

'No you didn't think at all!' Dad interrupted. 'What you did was extremely foolish and you deserve a curfew for the rest of your life!' Then Dad smiled. 'But I must say, I'm proud of you both.'

'Can we take food to him every day?' asked Jack.

'No, it's too dangerous. You two must promise to stay away from the woods - but I'll take it,' he answered.

'Oh, thank you, Dad!' said Jack, feeling very relieved that he wouldn't be punished and Dad would help.

The next morning Dad took some more bread and milk to the hide out, but the man was not there. He said that the prisoners had to work by day and were sometimes left to roam about the countryside at night, so maybe he would come back there to sleep that evening. Sure enough, the following day the food was gone. On the fourth day there was a little bunch of wild flowers where the food had been. Dad smiled. 'He's thanking us, I'll give them to Jane,' he said to himself. No one ever saw the man again and they always wondered what had happened to him, but they knew they had done something to help, and that felt very good indeed.

Chapter Thirteen

Happy Christmas Everyone!

It was nearly Christmas, the fifth Christmas since the German Occupation began and Dad was worried because life on the farm was getting very, very difficult. All through the war he had had plenty of food for his family, but now, if the war carried on for much longer, he wouldn't have enough to give them.

'We'll manage somehow,' said Mum, putting her arms round his neck.

'Yes, I suppose you're right,' he replied, giving her a kiss. 'You're amazing, Jane. You make flour from potatoes, drinks out of nettles and acorns, and wash our clothes without soap. I really don't know how you do it!'

'Well, you know what Maman always says?' she said, looking up at him.

'Make do and mend, there's always a way!' they said together, and both started to laugh.

But everything did get harder. The inspectors searched the farm again and again and took rabbits, chickens, pigs, potatoes and wheat and that made Dad mad!

'They say that they're giving it to the hungry people in the town, but I'm sure they're keeping most of it for themselves,' he said with a sigh. Jack was puzzled.

'Why do the soldiers need our food, Dad? I thought they always had enough to eat,' he asked.

'Well, Jack, now that the British Army has freed France from the Germans, the Germans can't get their supplies to the island, so they're as hungry as everyone else,' Dad explained.

Then one morning, when Lizzie went to feed the rabbits she had a terrible shock. They had all gone.

'Dad! Quick, come here!' she yelled, staring at the empty cages with their broken doors. Dad ran out to see what all the fuss was about.

'Oh no! What will they steal next?' he said angrily.

It seemed that every day something else vanished from their farm or the farms nearby. A barrel of potatoes had disappeared from the shed; three of Mr Le Brun's chickens had been stolen and Mrs Amy's cat was missing, probably shot and eaten. No one knew whether it was soldiers, starving prisoners or hungry Jersey folk who had stolen them.

'I'm going to leave my turkeys in the attic all the time. I don't want the Germans having them for dinner,' Maman told Mum, as she carried the ugly looking birds up the stairs.

'And I'll put some more potatoes and vegetables in the cellar for safe keeping,' Mum replied.

'But we must try to enjoy Christmas, German Occupation or not!' Maman called from the attic.

'I agree. We won't let the enemy spoil our day!' called back Mum.

'Are Uncle Frank and Aunt Emily coming to stay for Christmas?' asked Lizzie, who was sitting at the table doing her homework.

'Yes, they were delighted to be asked. Dad will collect them on Christmas Eve,' said Mum.

'And can we invite Miss Benest as well? Her family evacuated to England so she might be alone,' said

Lizzie.

'What a good idea. That teacher of yours is such fun,' replied Mum, giving her daughter a hug. 'You know, Lizzie, I think we'll all have a very happy time.'

The following week, everyone was very busy making presents for their family. Poppa disappeared into a small shed behind the barn and could be heard sawing and hammering.

'Don't you dare peek inside!' he said sternly. They were very curious and wondered what he was up to. It was very mysterious.

Maman cut up an old table cloth and sat at her treadle sewing machine stitching an apron for Mum and one for Aunt Emily. Dad put some homemade cider into a bottle for Uncle Frank and Lizzie unravelled a jumper that had belonged to Thomas and knitted two tiny hats for Maman and Mum.

'They're to put over their boiled eggs to keep them warm,' she explained to Jack. Mum cut up a torn pillowcase and made two hankies out of it, then she embroidered a flower in the corner of each.

'I'll give one to Miss Benest and one to Maman,' she told Dad. 'And I'll fill this pretty little biscuit tin with old buttons for Lizzie.'

Dad mended a small wooden box and covered it

with pictures from a comic book. 'Jack can keep his toy soldiers in here,' he said. They were all very pleased with what they had made. Only Jack and Charles could not think of anything to give the family.

Maman was always a bit sad on Christmas Eve, as one of her turkeys was to be eaten for Christmas dinner. Although she knew that farm animals were usually killed and eaten, she had looked after them for so long that she was sorry to have to say goodbye.

'We're lucky to have such good food,' she said with a sigh. Poppa took her hand and gently patted it. 'I understand. You really love your turkeys just like I loved my pigeons,' he said.

Maman smiled. 'Yes, I suppose you're right,'

Out in the garden, Jack helped Dad saw a branch off a fir tree to use as a Christmas tree.

'We're not really allowed to take branches off the trees,' said Dad.

'Why not? It's our tree,' said Jack,

'I know, but there's another new rule saying that we can't even cut down our own trees anymore.'

'That's silly! How will we keep the stove burning to cook our food and keep us warm if we haven't got any wood?' asked Jack.

'We've enough wood to keep the stove lit, but we

can't light the fire in the sitting room, so we'll have to stay in the kitchen for Christmas this year,' Dad explained, as he carried the branch into the kitchen and put it in a bucket in the corner of the room.

Mum got the box of Christmas decorations from the attic and began to decorate their tree, while Lizzie sat making snowmen and robins from scraps of newspaper. As Jack arranged their little wooden nativity set on the windowsill, he remembered Thomas playing with the cows and sheep and putting baby Jesus in the manger. He felt sad and still really missed his little brother.

Later that day, Dad and Jack went to town in the cart. Dad brought Chestnut to a halt outside Miss Benest's house just as she opened her door.

She was tall and thin, with thick red hair tied up in a large bun and fixed with a very big yellow bow. She wore a long brown and orange skirt, an orange jumper, had a green cape flung over her shoulders and carried a large tapestry bag covered with pictures of birds and flowers.

'Good afternoon, John, and hello there, Jack,' she said, as Dad helped her into the cart. 'Thank you so much for your kind invitation. What a lovely time we're going to have!'

Miss Benest smiled at Jack and he smiled back. She

reminded him of a tree in springtime; everything about her seemed bright and hopeful. He agreed that it really would be a very good Christmas.

Further down the street they stopped outside Uncle Frank's shop and soon he and Aunt Emily came outside.

'I don't know why I bother to lock the door,' said Uncle Frank with a sigh. 'The shelves in the shop are nearly empty, so there's not much left to steal in there.'

'You're right, but we mustn't worry about all that now,' said Aunt Emily. 'Come on, Frank, let's go!'

When they reached the farm, all the grownups sat by the stove chatting and laughing as they ate egg sandwiches and drank nettle tea. Charles, Lizzie and Jack took their sandwiches upstairs, sat on the floor in Lizzie's bedroom and played card games until their candle burnt out and they had to go to bed.

The next morning, Jack and Scratch rushed into the kitchen.

'Happy Christmas, Mum!' he said cheerfully.

'Happy Christmas, Jack,' Mum replied, giving him a kiss as he passed by. He ran into the yard shouting 'Happy Christmas, everyone!'

'And Happy Christmas to you, son,' came Dad's

reply from the stable. 'I've nearly finished milking the cows, so if you hurry up and feed the hens, we can all have breakfast together.'

Jack fed corn to the hens and then returned to the kitchen. It was a very busy place. Aunt Emily and Lizzie were peeling the potatoes and parsnips and Miss Benest was singing loudly as she chopped the carrots. Mum was making an apple pie and Maman had the turkey cooking in the oven. No one mentioned the turkey, but the smell was wonderful and Jack's mouth watered as he thought about their dinner.

Soon everything was ready and breakfast was over, so they all walked to the church in the village for the Christmas service. They sang carols and heard the story of baby Jesus, who was born in a stable and the shepherds and wise men who came to worship him. They met their friends and wished them a happy Christmas, and a new year that they all hoped would bring freedom from the enemy.

By the time they got home, they were very hungry and excited and what a feast they had! After dinner, Dad took a piece of paper out of his pocket.

'Quiet everyone! I've got some very special news for you all,' he said. 'This is a note from Uncle Bill; it was posted nearly two years ago but only arrived yesterday.

It just says that they are all safe and well.'

'What a wonderful surprise! That has made my day!' said Maman, clapping her hands with happiness.

'Thank goodness they're safe. I really hope their next letter won't take as long to reach us,' said Mum as she wiped the tears from her eyes.

Jack was really pleased to hear from Simon and his family and hoped that they were enjoying Christmas as much as he was, but he wondered whether he would ever see his cousin again.

Charles decided to get out some cards for everyone to play. 'Here you are, how about playing some games?' he said, putting them down on the table.

'We have to wash the dishes first,' answered Mum.

'No, you stay there, Aunt Jane. Jack and I haven't got any presents to give you, so we've decided to do the dishes for you today,' Charles replied.

'Well, that's as good as any present could be! Thank you so much boys,' Mum said. So Jack and Charles washed and scrubbed and dried the dishes, while the others laughed and joked as they played Snap and Happy Families.

Eventually the dishes were done and Lizzie gave out the presents. As well as those they had made for each other, Mum had exchanged two jars of jam for a pair of wooden clogs for Dad. Everyone laughed as he clomped around the kitchen making Scratch bark and growl at the noisy wooden shoes.

Aunt Emily gave Mum a small piece of soap that she had kept from before the war. 'Happy Christmas, and thank you for having Charles to stay on the farm,' she said.

'Oh thank you, Emily!' Mum exclaimed. 'I'd almost forgotten what real soap looked like.'

'And this is for you, son,' Uncle Frank said to Charles, handing him a penknife with two shiny blades.

'But it's yours, Dad,' Charles said, turning it round in his hands and opening up the blades.

'No, it's yours now,' answered his father. Charles thought it was the best present he had ever had.

'What about me?' Have you all forgotten your poor old Poppa?' Poppa said, pretending to cry.

'Of course not, you silly old man!' answered Maman, as she gave him a package wrapped in a small blue cloth. Inside were five cigarettes and a small tin of tobacco. 'Where did you get them from?' he asked in surprise.

'Never you mind,' Maman answered. She didn't want to tell him that this time she had exchanged her favourite scarf for his gift.

Then, at last, it was Poppa's turn to give his present. Everyone followed him into the yard wondering what it could be.

'You wait there,' he ordered, looking very pleased with himself. He disappeared into his little shed and soon reappeared pushing his surprise into the yard. It was covered in an old blanket and looked very mysterious.

'Is it a rocking chair for Maman?' shouted Jack.

'Or a plane for us to escape to England in!' said Dad, and they all began to laugh.

'Come on Poppa, hurry up! Show us, please,' shouted Jack excitedly.

'Here you are,' he said, throwing off the blanket. 'Happy Christmas everyone!'

'Oh Poppa,' exclaimed Lizzie as she went to look more closely. 'Is this really for us?'

'Of course it is!' he replied. 'Well, do you like it then?'

'It's wonderful,' Lizzie answered, throwing her arms round her grandfather's neck and giving him a big, big kiss. 'Thank you Poppa.'

Jack just stood and stared. There in front of him was the best go-cart he had ever seen. It was made from the wheels off Thomas's pram; the seat from a broken chair; bits of wood from the old fence at the corner of the yard and a piece of rope that had been used to tether the cows.

Miss Benest clapped her hands, 'Oh how splendid! Come on then, who'll be first to have a ride?'

'Me!' shouted Jack, Lizzie and Charles all at once, as they all tried to get onto the seat.

'One at a time, please,' said Dad. 'Boys, you push Lizzie for a while.' Lizzie grasped hold of the rope and they gave her a big push, which sent the go-cart whizzing across the yard. 'Push me again!' she shouted and off they went again with Scratch barking and chasing after them.

They were so excited that they didn't notice when Miss Benest quietly crept back into the house. She went upstairs and put a little envelope, made out of bright purple material, on everyone's pillow. Inside each was a smooth, round pebble on which she had painted a message. Jack's said, 'Keep Smiling'. Lizzie's said, 'Be Happy'. Everyone's message was special.

That evening they sang Christmas carols until they went upstairs to bed, where they found one more present on their pillows. Jack and Lizzie thought it was a wonderful end to their Christmas day, but Mum and Dad lay in bed wondering what the new year would bring.

'Things are going to get even harder you know, Jane,' said Dad. 'There's hardly any food left and we're running out of wood too.'

'Do you think the war will end soon?' asked Mum.

'I hope so,' answered Dad, giving her a kiss. 'I don't think anyone can manage for much longer.'

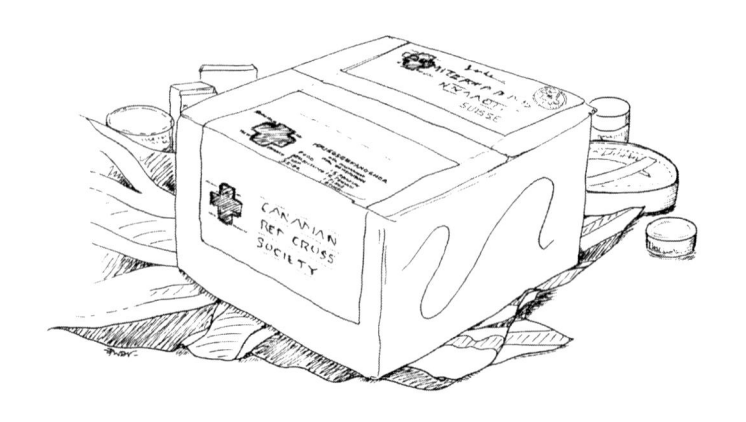

Chapter Fourteen

We're Free!

It was January 1945 and there was very good news. The Germans allowed a Red Cross ship called the S.S. *Vega* to bring food parcels for everyone. It docked at the harbour and hundreds of excited people watched as thousands of boxes were unloaded onto the pier.

Dad and Charles took the van to town to pick up parcels for people in their village, while the town people went to collect their own. There were men balancing boxes on bicycles; women pushing prams and wheelbarrows filled with boxes for their families and children struggling to carry their precious parcel home.

'This has come just in time,' said Dad. 'These people would have died soon without this food.'

Back at the farm, the family eagerly waited for Dad and Charles to return. There was a parcel for everyone containing things they hadn't seen for years.

'Look! Chocolate!' shouted Lizzie, holding up a small bar.

'Don't eat it all at once, Lizzie,' said Mum.

'Oh a tin of salmon. That's my favourite!' said Poppa.

Maman laughed and clapped her hands. 'I've got soap in my box. It will be so good to have a proper wash tonight!' and she popped it into her pocket for safe keeping.

Mum put all the butter, sugar, marmalade, salmon, sardines, prunes, ham, corned beef, milk powder, cheese, salt and pepper into the larder.

'We don't know when we'll get another parcel so we mustn't eat it all at once,' she said. Then she picked up her bag of tea and box of biscuits. 'But I think we should have a proper tea party today don't you?' She got her very best china cups and saucers, plates and matching teapot out from the dresser and the family sat around the table waiting for the first cup of real tea they had had in years. When it had brewed, Mum put a little milk in each cup and poured the tea in too.

'Well Maman, you'll enjoy this!' said Dad, passing her a cup and watching as she slowly sipped the hot tea and licked her lips.

'Ooh! That's good!' she said with a smile.

Over the next few months, the S.S. *Vega* brought more parcels for the hungry islanders and the food saved the lives of many people. But back on the farm, more and more of Dad's crops were taken away. Even the seed potatoes he had planted in the fields were dug up and eaten by hungry Germans and their prisoners. Soon there were no seeds left in the island, so the farmers couldn't grow the food people would need.

'We need to find some new hiding places for our food, just in case the inspector finds the cellar,' said Dad. 'Have you got any ideas?'

'What about hiding it under the straw in the barn?' suggested Lizzie.

'No darling, I'm sure he would look there.'

'We could put some potatoes in a tin and bury it in the woods,' said Jack.

Dad thought for a moment. 'That's a very good idea. Come on, let's do it!'

They found some old tins and filled one with potatoes, one with carrots and another with some butter Mum had made by shaking milk in a bottle. When Dad was sure that no one was watching, they went into the woods, where Jack dug a hole under his oak tree and buried his box. Then Dad made a hole near the stream and Lizzie put her tin in the ground under a holly bush. She got pricked and scratched but didn't really mind, 'No one will look here,' she thought.

They all carefully covered the boxes with soil and leaves and soon everything looked just the way it had before.

'Job done!' said Dad, as they walked back to the farm. 'Who would have thought that we'd behave like the squirrels, hiding things away like that!'

'We've hidden our boxes,' said Jack when he got indoors. 'Mum, I'm hungry now; can I have some bread and jam please?'

'Sorry, Jack, not today, we haven't got any bread left at all.'

Jack frowned. 'We've got plenty of potato flour in the cellar, can't you bake some more?'

'No, it's not safe, Jack. If soldiers come into the yard and smell bread baking in the oven, then they will know that we had hidden some flour from them. We can't take that risk.' Jack sighed; he really was fed up with the inspectors now!

Then one cold frosty afternoon, Poppa came into the kitchen looking very worried.

'Maman won't get out of bed, Jane,' he said. 'She has stayed there all day and I don't know what's wrong with her.' Mum rushed to the cottage and found Maman curled up under her blankets.

'What's wrong, Maman?' she asked, sitting down beside her.

'I'm so tired and cold,' she answered, her voice shaky and sad. 'We have to work so hard and my old bones ache. I just want to stay in bed.' Mum took her hand.

'Don't worry, we'll look after you,' she said. Then, as she walked back to the farmhouse, she had an idea.

'I think Maman and Poppa need to move into the farmhouse with us,' she said when she told Dad what had happened. Dad nodded.

'Yes, I agree. We can put a bed in the kitchen near the stove so that Maman keeps warm, Poppa can have Jack's room and Jack will have to share with Charles.

Poppa was very relieved and thankful that he had such a loving family to help him and Maman soon felt much better. She sat up in bed and told everyone what to do, but they didn't mind, it was good to see her well and happy again.

Then one day, when mum was putting a chicken onto a tray ready to cook for their dinner and Maman was sitting in bed darning Dad's socks, they heard German voices in the yard.

'The chicken! Where can we hide it?' Mum exclaimed, picking up the tray. 'Oh dear! We didn't tell them about this one so we shouldn't have kept it.'

'Quick, put it in my bed,' suggested Maman, 'I'll pretend to be really ill, then they won't make me move.' So they put the chicken under the covers, Maman lay down and shut her eyes and Mum sat by her bedside. Soon a soldier came into the room and saw the sick old woman.

'Good morning,' Mum whispered, as if Maman was asleep and she did not want to wake her.

'Good morning,' the soldier replied. 'I'm sorry the lady is sick, we will not disturb you.' And with that, he went back into the yard. Mum held her breath and waited.

'They've gone!' said Maman, opening her eyes and laughing. 'Well, I think you can have this chicken back again, Jane. You know, it was fun to do my bit against the enemy!'

When the family sat around the table that evening,

they all laughed and laughed as they imagined the scene. They also enjoyed every mouthful of chicken knowing that it was one less for the Germans to eat!

A few days later, as Mum peeled some apples, there was a knock on the door. 'I hope it's not the soldiers again,' she said to Maman. But this time, there was nothing to hide, so she went to see who it was.

'Hello Ani! It's so nice to see you, come in, come in,' she said. Ani followed her into the kitchen and burst into tears.

'What is it, love?' asked Mum.

'We've finished the food that was in our last parcel and we don't have anything left. Can you help us?' she sobbed.

'Come here,' said Mum, putting her arms around the thin, crying girl. 'Let me get you a glass of milk, then we'll see what we can do.'

Ani sat down by the stove and warmed her hands. 'It's really cold in our cottage, we haven't got enough wood to make a fire. Mum is so sad and hungry that she just stays in bed all the time and cries,' she explained.

'Shhh, Ani, I'll visit your mother and suggest that you both come here for dinner each day. We haven't got much, but if you bring your rations too, I'm sure we can give you a good meal.'

'Oh thank you!' Ani cried, tears falling down her cheeks again.

So every day, Ani and her mother came to the farm to eat with the family. As soon as dinner was finished, they walked home again with full tummies, ready to face whatever the day would bring.

Winter passed and spring arrived, the hedges were covered with flowers and the birds were singing, but nothing seemed to change in Jersey. In fact, Jack thought the rules and orders were getting worse.

One night he was upset and very angry. Everything seemed to be going wrong! It was only eight o'clock and he and Charles had to go to bed because they had completely run out of candles. But worst of all, he had been told to keep Scratch indoors (unless they were out together), because the soldiers were shooting dogs and eating them.

'If they shoot Scratch, I'll kill them!' he said angrily, thumping his pillow with his fist.

Charles laughed. 'I'd like to see you try!'

'It's not funny. I hate them!' Jack replied.

'Yes, me too,' said Charles, wondering if there was anything they could do to make life difficult for the enemy. 'Why don't you come with me to cut the telephone wires leading to Belle Vue?' he suggested, 'then the soldiers won't be able to contact the headquarters in the town.'

'Do you think we could do it without being seen?' Jack asked.

'We could try. What do you think?'

'Good idea,' said Jack, feeling too angry to be scared. A few hours later, when everyone was asleep, the two boys crept out into the yard. The moon appeared from behind the clouds and they were able to see just enough to go up the drive into the lane. They moved silently, listening for any unusual sounds. When they reached the telephone pole in the hedge near Belle Vue, everything was quiet and still.

'Hide up there,' whispered Charles, pointing to a nearby tree that was covered with leaves. 'Keep a watch out and whistle once if you see anyone coming.'

Jack climbed into the tree and Charles slowly climbed up the pole. He took out his pliers and quickly cut through the wires before sliding down to the ground again.

'Come on, let's get home,' he said, feeling very pleased with what he had done.

The next day there was a notice in the Evening Post anyone caught cutting wires would be shot! They had had a very lucky escape.

Jack was now allowed to join the adults as they listened to the news on their wireless, and the news got better and better. They heard that the Germans were losing the war, and best of all was the news that Hitler was dead!

Then one day, as Jack played with Scratch in the woods, he heard a plane flying overhead. He ran to the old oak tree and climbed high into its branches. From there, he could see the small plane flying low over the island. It was painted grey and yellow, with red, white and blue circles on its wings. 'That's a British plane,' he told Scratch, as he jumped down and hugged his collie dog friend. Scratch looked up at him and barked as if he understood. 'I'm sure the British will rescue us very soon. Let's go home and tell everyone.'

Two days later, when Jack, Lizzie and Charles were playing cards in the kitchen, they heard loud shouts coming from the attic.

'What's going on?' exclaimed Lizzie in surprise.

'I don't know,' Jack replied. 'Come on, let's go and find out.' They ran up the stairs and stood, open-mouthed at the attic door. Poppa was hugging Maman, shouting 'we've won, we've won,' and Mum and Dad were laughing and doing a little dance.

'Dad, what are you doing?' shouted Lizzie at the

top of her voice. Dad stopped and grinned.

'Listen,' he said, and to their surprise, they could hear the wireless with good news coming from London. 'We've won, Lizzie. The war is over. Germany has been defeated. What wonderful news!'

'Come here,' said Mum, pulling her children towards her. 'Can you believe it? The war is over!'

'And we can take down the picture!' shouted Jack excitedly.

'That picture!' exclaimed Lizzie. 'Can you tell me about it now?' Jack grinned.

'Not yet, but I'll tell you very soon!' he replied.

That night, no one wanted to go to bed. They talked and laughed and imagined what would happen when the British landed. They wondered when Uncle Bill and Aunt May would return to their farm and Maman said that they probably wouldn't even recognise Clare and Simon because they would have grown so much.

Eventually they said goodnight, but Jack couldn't sleep. He felt strange – a mixture of excitement, sadness and worry too. He was excited that the British were coming to free them, but he thought about his little brother, Thomas, and felt sad that he was not there to celebrate with the family. As he stroked Scratch, who was sitting on the floor beside his bed, he worried that when Simon returned to Jersey, he would have to give Scratch back to him, and he really didn't want to do that. He tossed and turned and only when Scratch jumped onto his bed and snuggled down with him, did he fall into a dreamless sleep.

The next day, the soldiers looked miserable and wandered about not knowing what to do. The islanders were not scared of them anymore and began to celebrate by wearing red, white and blue ribbons on their clothes or in their hair and taking their Union Jacks out of their hiding places, ready to hoist high on the flag poles as soon as the British arrived.

At school, everyone was very excited and Mrs Gray beamed at her class.

'Children, you have been just wonderful! Times have been hard but we've stuck together.' She went and tapped the picture of the sailing boat with the secret still hidden behind it. 'Very soon we'll throw this old boat away!' she said, laughing at their happy faces.

'Hooray,' shouted the children, clapping their hands and hugging each other. They all knew exactly what she meant!

Just then, Mr Richardson came into the room. He was smiling too and had more good news.

'We've just been told to close the school for the rest

of the day. All go home; you and your families might want to go into St Helier to watch the British arrive. The next time I see you, we'll be free!'

Jack rushed into the playground where he found Lizzie and together they ran all the way back to the farm.

'The school closed,' explained Lizzie, 'can we go into town, Dad, please, please?' she begged, jumping up and down with joy.

'What about going with Charles to Uncle Frank's house, then you'll see all that's going on. We'll join you tomorrow,' he replied.

So Jack, Lizzie and Charles set off for the town. There were no buses but they were happy to walk, joining the crowds all eager to see the British sailors land at the harbour. People laughed and sang while silent German soldiers watched in dismay. They reached the Royal Square just as the clock struck three. A wireless was switched on, and through loudspeakers tied to the lamp posts, they heard a voice. Everyone went quiet and Winston Churchill, the Prime Minister in England, began to speak.

'Our dear Channel Islands are also to be freed today,' he said, in his slow gruff voice. Everyone cheered and cheered. Someone began to sing the national anthem and soon everyone in the square was joining in and singing 'God save our gracious King. Long live our noble King. God save the King', at the top of their voices.

'Come on, let's go home and find Mum and Dad,' said Charles, pulling Jack and Lizzie through the crowd. They went down the road to the shop, which now had a large Union Jack in the window. Uncle Frank and Aunt Emily were very pleased to see them.

'What an exciting day!' they said.

Early next morning, Dad arrived with his van pulled by Chestnut and Robin, who looked splendid with ribbons tied to their manes. Maman sat in her armchair, which was securely tied onto the back of the van, watching all that was going on, while Poppa sat on a bale of straw waving at the happy crowd. Then they all headed down to the bay to join the hundreds of people who were waiting for the British to come.

Suddenly a warship sailed into view. There was a very loud cheer - this was the moment everyone had been waiting for. Maman put out her arms and began to cry and Poppa shook his head and rubbed his eyes, wondering whether it was all a dream. Dad threw his cap into the air and grabbed hold of Mum, swinging her round and giving her a hug,

Then a smaller boat sailed towards the harbour, so Jack, Charles and Lizzie pushed their way through the cheering crowd and hurried back to the pier. They climbed onto the sea wall and watched as the first British sailors landed to liberate the island.

There were people everywhere and the sailors were picked up and carried high on peoples' shoulders. They waved and threw sweets into the happy crowd and everyone wanted to touch them and thank them for coming to their rescue. Suddenly, Jack noticed a young sailor with very fair hair.

'Look at the sailor on that man's shoulders. I think it's Michael from our village,' he shouted.

'It is, it is! Lizzie replied excitedly. 'Michael, over here!' she yelled, waving as hard as she could to get his attention.

Michael turned, spotted them in the crowd and waved back. How proud he felt to be one of the first British sailors to land on his island.

That afternoon, after all meeting up again at Uncle Frank's shop, Poppa and Maman sat at an upstairs window and watched all that was going on. The rest of the family went back to the harbour, where they stood with the crowd, eyes fixed on the balcony of the Pomme d'Or Hotel.

Suddenly, a British Officer appeared and spoke to the crowd and the huge Nazi flag that had flown there since the Occupation began, was taken down. As the Union Jack was raised again, everyone cheered, church bells rang and people proudly sang the national anthem. It was May 9th 1945 and the British were back!

'Well, the Occupation really is over,' shouted Dad, trying to be heard above the noise.

'At last!' Mum replied, looking at her husband, 'I hardly know what we should do now!' she said.

'Come back to the shop with me, I've got a little surprise,' said Uncle Frank mysteriously. So they pushed and shoved through the crowd again, were kissed and hugged by complete strangers and eventually got back to the shop. Once inside, Uncle Frank disappeared into the attic and returned with an old tin box.

'I kept these hidden away to be used only on liberation day,' he said, taking out five long fireworks. 'Come on, let's celebrate!'

From the garden, they watched as the fireworks shot up into the sky and burst into silver stars that flew in all directions before fading away.

'Hooray! Hip, hip hooray,' they cried.

'We need to get back to the farm, the cows should have been milked an hour ago,' said Dad. 'But on an important day like this, I don't think they'll mind!' Everyone laughed and then Dad went to collect the horses and van which he'd left in a small field just out of town. It was a very happy family that went home that day.

Jack helped Dad with the milking, as Charles had stayed with his parents. It felt rather strange to be doing an ordinary task on such a special occasion. When at last he went to bed, he couldn't wait for morning to come as he had a wonderful surprise for his family.

So the following morning, as Scratch bounded onto his bed as usual, Jack jumped up and dressed as quickly as he could.

'Quick, come on Scratch,' he called as he raced down the stairs into the kitchen.

'Mum, Dad, there's something we have to do!' he said excitedly, hopping from one foot to the other.

'Slow down, Jack,' said Dad. 'What's all this about?'

'You need to come to my classroom at school,' he replied.

'But we don't have to go to school today,' said Lizzie, who appeared at the door.

'I know, but it's important. I have something to show you, we all do,' he explained. Lizzie's eyes lit up.

'Is it something to do with that picture?' she asked.

'It might be,' Jack replied. 'Mrs Gray said that at nine o'clock on the day after the Germans surrendered, we should ask our families to come to the school.'

'This sounds very interesting,' said Dad, looking at his watch. 'Eat your breakfast and then we'll go.' Once breakfast was over, Jack raced into the yard.

'Hurry up! Hurry up!' he shouted impatiently. 'We mustn't be late. Come on!'

Mum laughed. 'Calm down, there's plenty of time,' she said, as she put her arms around him and gave him a great big kiss.

'I do love you, Jack,' she said. He giggled and wriggled out of her arms, suddenly remembering a time just before the Germans had occupied Jersey. He had heard the sound of bombs exploding on the coast of France and was frightened. He had found Mum in the garden and she had put her arms around him then. She had told him that whatever happened they would stay together and be just fine. She had kept her promise. He smiled.

'I love you too, Mum,' he said.

Just then, Scratch ran towards them, barking and wagging his tail. Lizzie had tied red, white and blue ribbons onto his collar and he was coming too.

Soon the family was walking up the lane towards the school. They met Richard with his parents and Lizzie ran to ask Ani to come too. When they reached the playground, Mr Richardson and Mrs Gray were standing on the steps waiting to welcome them.

'What a wonderful day this is!' said Mrs Gray.

'Woof!' went Scratch and everyone laughed.

'I'm glad you agree!' said Mrs Gray. 'Now, come on in everyone, you too Scratch, we have something to show you.' They all followed her into the classroom and the children proudly stood with her by the picture of the sailing ship.

'Throughout the occupation, the children and I have had a secret,' Mrs Gray explained. 'It's been a secret that we haven't shared with anyone, but a secret that has helped us stay hopeful that one day the war would end.' She smiled at the eager faces looking up at her. 'It's time to show your families, don't you think?'

'Yes, yes!' shouted the children.

Mrs Gray carefully removed the picture of the ship and revealed the photograph of their king – King George VI of England. The grownups gasped in surprise and clapped loudly. Then, just as she had promised, everyone stood to attention and sang the national anthem at the top of their voices. They all knew that their king would never have to be hidden again!

Later that morning, Mum, Dad, Lizzie, Jack and Scratch walked through the playground and stopped to look at the Union Jack that was flying from the flagpole. Dad put his big strong arms around his family.

'Well, it's hard to take it in. We really are free again,' he said, hugging them tight. 'Come on, let's go.' And they headed back to their farm, feeling safe at last in their island home.

Author's note

How I came to write *The King Behind the Picture:*

When I was growing up, my Mum and Dad often told me about their lives as children during the German Occupation of Jersey. I found this so interesting, that when I was training to be a teacher and had to write a very long essay, I decided to write about the boys and girls who grew up during the Occupation years.

I sent questionnaires to a hundred people who were children during that time, asking them what they did and how they felt, growing up with the Germans ruling their island. Many replied, sending me stories about life at home and at school. They described sad, frightening and funny things that happened to them and their families. I interviewed grown-ups who had important jobs to do during the war, read diaries kept by some primary school head teachers and also the *Evening Post*, which was printed every day throughout the war.

A few years ago, I realised that there were not many

stories written for children about the Occupation, so I collected together all the information I had and turned it into this book, which I hope you enjoyed.

The story itself is not true, but nearly everything that happens is based on memories and actual events.

Marianne Le Boutillier
September 2013